EVEREST

KINGS OF RETRIBUTION MC LOUISIANA

CRYSTAL DANIELS

SANDY ALVAREZ

TWO PENS-

CRYSTAL *Daniels*

Sandy ALVAREZ

-ONE STORY

1

EVEREST

I glance at the stars scattered across the expansive sky.

This place is barren, nothing more than dust and rock. It's a forgotten patch of hell, the devil's playground, where men like us come to do the dirty work others won't.

When I say *men like us*, I'm talking about the Riggs, Thors, Preachers, and Cowboys of the world. The ones who dive headfirst into the heart of chaos, living on the edge of life or death. Not to say that the MC lifestyle doesn't include all the same elements where danger is a constant companion, but for me, this mercenary shit is a first. For them, it's just another day in the office.

I run a hand over my jaw, scanning the terrain through the night vision scope, every breath feeling like inhaling sand. During the day, the heat is oppressive, dry, and relentless, the air smelling of scorched earth and sweat—nothing like Louisiana's thick humidity I've known over the years.

When night falls over the vast desert landscape, the air cools dramatically, transitioning from the day's scorching heat to a refreshing chill. As the landscape is swallowed by darkness, silence becomes palpable, broken only by the occasional murmurs from the men we've been sent here to take out.

We've been out here for three days, tracking, waiting, and barely sleeping. The mission is taking its toll with heat exhaustion, dehydration, and the constant weight of danger riding our backs. There isn't much around to keep us hidden from the enemy, just a bunch of rocks and sage bushes. We lost our shot at an ambush yesterday when one of the hostages was dragged out front and beaten bloody while the cartel recorded it. We had to sit, watching and holding our position, knowing that making a move would jeopardize not only the life of the man being brutally attacked but also the safety of the other hostages being held inside.

I roll my shoulders to ease the soreness. My body aches from pushing it far beyond anything I've done before, yet I welcome the feeling.

I've been craving something to jolt me out of the relentless funk I've been in, so when Wick had to bow out of the mission, I half-jokingly offered to take his place. To my surprise, Riggs took my offer seriously, and here I am.

It's not that I don't like my life, I do. I have the club and my brothers. I'm also involved with my community, giving back and helping the youth as much as possible. Yet, beneath all that lies a deep-seated desire for more. But I'm not sure what *more* is just yet.

Hunkered down in the dirt, rifle locked and loaded, I tell myself that this is what I signed up for—a challenge and a chance to chase the high it gives me.

"Two gunmen at the front. A couple more on the east and west sides of the villa," Preacher's voice crackles through my earpiece, low and steady, breaking through my thoughts. "Could be more around back," he adds.

I adjust my grip, shifting against the uneven ground and loose rock. The abandoned compound sprawls out in front of us, an old stone villa used as a makeshift fortress in the middle of nowhere, surrounded by rusted-out vehicles and barbed wire. The bastards inside, members of the cartel, have five hostages, three women and two men, high value, names classified. This mission is a government job. All we know is that a covert operation went south, and the cartel retaliated. And if we don't get them out, their next stop is a shallow grave, or worse, knowing what these men are capable of.

Riggs kneels beside me, his gaze locked on the compound. "Intel says they want a prisoner exchange, and they want all DEA and CIA operations targeting them shut down. We don't move soon, and those motherfuckers start sending body parts to prove they mean business."

"What's the plan?" I ask, scanning the compound's layout for the hundredth time.

"The compound is sealed tighter than a gnat's ass," Riggs says. "They have men at every entry point. Sneaking in isn't just difficult, it's damn near impossible," he says in a low, tense voice, the weight of the situation clear in his tone. "Our window of opportunity is closing. Our only option is to go in quickly, aggressively, and hope like hell we kill them before they kill the hostages or us."

"We've been through worse," Thor whispers.

The fact that we're stepping into the unknown heightens the tension.

Nearby, Cowboy lets out a measured exhale as he methodically checks his rifle. "Good thing we've got a few surprises of our own." He grins confidently, patting a tan-colored pack strapped securely to his back, which also has a miniature grenade launcher. "What do ya say we show these knob gobblers what we're made of?"

I smirk. If there's one thing I've learned over the years from being with the club and spending time with Cowboy, Thor, and

Preacher is the fact that they thrive in chaos, relishing the hunt as they wipe out humanity's scum with ruthless precision.

They also enjoy blowing shit up.

Another adrenaline rush floods my veins, and tension crackles in the air, paired with an insatiable hunger for action. We all know what's at stake, and lives are on the line. There's no room for hesitation, no time for second-guessing. You either embrace the chaos or you get left behind.

Riggs signals, and a stillness washes over me as we silently move. A faint breeze rattles loose panels of corrugated metal used for fencing surrounding the villa. The distant sound of muffled voices becomes louder as we close in. So far, the cartel is oblivious to the death moving toward them.

We fan out.

I move in on a target.

My pulse slows.

My breaths are steady.

The motherfucker never sees me coming.

One second, he's scanning the darkness, the next, my arm is locking around his throat, cutting off his airway. He claws at my forearm, attempting to break free. The only sound he makes is a choked gurgle before his body goes limp. I lower his lifeless body silently to the ground and press forward, coming up on Thor, swiftly extinguishing the life of another target, leaving the corpse slumped over a metal barrel.

A few yards away is another cartel member, his rifle hanging at his side, taking a piss. I pull my knife from the sheath strapped to my thigh, the blade gleaming in the moonlight. I move in, slow and steady. The bastard doesn't sense me, oblivious to the fact that death is breathing down his neck. My finger tightens around the knife's hilt, its weight familiar and comforting.

One step.

Then another.

I hold my breath.

And strike fast.

My hand clamps over his mouth, yanking his head back against my chest. He struggles and tries to scream, but all that comes out is a muffled grunt against my palm while fumbling for his rifle, which falls to the ground. Desperate, his fingers claw at my wrist, but I've got the strength. My blade slides deep across his throat, hot blood spilling over my hand. His body shudders, then goes slack in my grip. Careful not to make a sound, I lower him to the ground and hover over him. His eyes are wide, full of terror, but there's no life left in the motherfucker, just a few last, wet gasps as he stares up at me before the light goes out. I exhale and stand, wiping the blade clean against my pants.

"Positions?" Riggs' voice crackles through the earpiece.

"East side," Preacher replies with a steadiness in his tone.

"West side," Cowboy responds.

"South end," I state, indicating my position.

"South," Thor murmurs, confirming his location.

"I've got the front entrance secured," Riggs asserts confidently, his voice steady and authoritative. After a brief pause, he continues, "Strike first. Strike hard and leave nothing standin'."

"Do or die, no in-between," Thor proclaims.

Cowboy chuckles low. "Let's kick the dust off and light a fire."

"Let God judge the man, but first we send them to meet him," Preacher adds.

A heavy silence lingers for a heartbeat, each thump of my pulse echoing in my ears. "Let's make the devil sweat," I add.

"Hell yeah. Let's move," Riggs orders, and I raise my rifle, heading for one of the exit points at the back of the crumbling villa.

Thor steps up and, with small precision tools, starts working on the heavy, rusty padlock—a sharp click and then silence.

A voice drifts from inside. "Time's up. Make the call and tell them we're starting with one of the women." His accent is thick.

Thor looks at me. "Ready?"

I nod.

Then raise my rifle, finger firm on the trigger, and without hesitation, enter.

The first man we encounter barely gets a breath before my bullet punches through his skull, slamming his body against the wall and leaving a smear of blood as his body slides down.

A second motherfucker reacts, his hands reaching for his weapon. Thor kills him with two rounds to the chest, his body jerking before crumbling to the floor.

All hell breaks loose, and the compound erupts in a mix of shouting and gunfire.

A bullet whizzes past my ear as we enter another room. Another burns as it rips a line across the top of my shoulder, but I press forward.

Across the room, Riggs meets a charging man head-on, deflecting a machete's blade and then slamming the bastard's head into the wall so hard it bursts like a dropped melon. He looks around. "Move."

Thor, Riggs, and I step over the dead, exiting the room.

"We've located the hostages," Preacher says into the earpiece, his voice steady.

"Where?" Riggs barks.

"End of hall, from your location," Cowboy replies.

At the end of the hall, just outside the door of another room, Cowboy has his rifle trained on a cartel member, and I'm wondering why he hasn't put a bullet in his head yet.

"You've just dug your own graves," the cartel member spits at him as we approach.

I pause, looking at the bastard. "Good thing dirt doesn't care whose corpse it is," I tell the motherfucker then watch with satisfaction as Cowboy pulls the trigger.

When we enter the room, we find Riggs and Preacher helping the now-rescued climb out of a hole in the floor. But with them are extra warm bodies—three young girls who can't be any older than their teens. My stomach coils.

"Underground tunnels. Most likely used for drug smugglers and skin traders," Preacher states, the beam of his flashlight shining down into the dark hole, looking for others.

As I watch the group huddle together, my chest tightens at the sight of the three girls. Their fear is palpable and suffocating. Their wide eyes dart around like startled deer. I notice how they cling to each other, their knuckles white. I know the dark truth of the situation and the horrors that awaited all of them. The thought ignites a fierce burning in my chest, and I clench my fists tightly. "They touch any of you?" I ask, my voice laced with concern.

"No," the brunette reassures me, her eyes wide as she and the blonde—both older—shield the young girls.

"Let's get the fuck out of here. The extraction point is half a mile north," Riggs says with urgency.

We gather the rescues and work our way out, Preacher helping the beaten man walk out of the building. My boots pound against the dry, cracked ground as we leave the old villa behind us and scan our surroundings, my eyes adjusting again to the endless void of black.

"Pick up the pace," Cowboy barks, his voice tight. "We got about sixty seconds before we see fireworks."

The rescues attempt to pick up the pace, but exhaustion drags them down. One of the women nearly trips, but Thor hauls her up without breaking his stride.

"Keep movin'," Riggs snaps, glancing over his shoulder.

An eerie stillness in the air makes the hair on the back of my neck rise.

Then, the night erupts.

The villa explodes in a massive fireball, followed by a shockwave that feels like it passes through my body. The roar is deafening, causing my ears to ring. Heat soon follows, even from this distance, a wave of scorching air carrying the stench of burning stone, wood, and flesh. The flames light up the night sky with shades of orange and red as plumes of thick black smoke coil upward, turning the night into a battlefield.

Preacher coughs, waving his hand in front of his face as the burnt smell thickens. "I think I just inhaled one of them dead cartel motherfuckers."

"Incoming!" Cowboy shouts from behind, and we look over our shoulders. Barely visible through the smoke-choked darkness, headlights slice through.

"Fuck! Get down!" Riggs barks at the rescues, and they drop, covering their heads, the women and men shielding the girls.

I keep my eyes locked on the vehicle barreling straight toward us. Then gunfire rips through the dark, bullets pelting the ground.

"Where the hell did they come from?" Thor shouts.

Cowboy drops to one knee, shoulders the small grenade launcher he's been itching to use, and lines up his shot. The thump of the launcher barely registers before the truck explodes, sending metal shards into the air while sending another shockwave rattling through my chest.

"Move, move, move!" Riggs barks, and everyone is up and pushing forward.

We reach the extraction point as the deep *whoosh-whomp* of helicopter blades cuts through the night. The rotor kicks up a storm of sand and grit, stinging the skin on my face as we load the rescues into the chopper, putting us right at max capacity. The second the door slides shut, the pilot lifts off. My stomach lurches, gravity pulling hard on my body before we level out. The smell of sweat, blood, and spent gunpowder clings to my clothes, and adrenaline still thrums in my veins as a heavy breath leaves my body.

I shift in my seat, scanning the people packed in the chopper. Preacher is across from me, his rifle cradled across his chest. Cowboy is next to him, head tilted back, eyes closed. Thor is at the door, his eyes looking out the window. Riggs is at my side, his usual controlled energy humming under the surface.

I glance at our rescues. They're weary and exhausted but alive, and that's what matters.

The ride stretches on, nothing but the pulse of the rotors breaking the stillness. I finally let my head fall against the metal interior, staring at the bolts and panels above me.

"You handled yourself like a soldier out there." Riggs' voice cuts through the hum of the chopper. "Damn glad I brought you along." There's no bullshit in his words, no empty praise, just pride in his tone.

Something tightens in my chest, something I don't have words for, so I nod, hoping that's enough.

After landing at another secure location, the rescued are loaded into a passenger van. The brunette steps forward, her face streaked with dirt and sweat. She makes sure to lock eyes with each of us. "Those girls are why I continue to do what I do, regardless of the danger I put myself in." She looks back at the van and then at us again. "I just wanted to say thank you."

Thor wipes sweat from his brow. "You gotta name, beautiful?" He cocks his head, flashing her a smile.

"That's classified," she says.

Thor places a hand over his heart like she just shot him. "Damn. Does that mean your number is classified too?" he teases, and she smiles a little.

"Afraid so." She turns and climbs into the van, closing the door.

Cowboy snorts as the vehicle drives away. "You'd flirt with a rattlesnake if it batted its eyelashes at you," he tells Thor.

"I thrive on danger." Thor chuckles with a confident grin.

Riggs strides over to us. "Listen up, everyone! Just got off the line with Wick. He and Tequila are about to welcome their little one into the world." He shoots a broad grin at Cowboy, Thor, and Preacher. "Ya'll up for another trip?"

The three look at each other, and then Cowboy answers, "Let the good times roll!"

We all climb in the chopper and when we land in Louisiana, we're running on fumes, but there is no time to waste. We tear through the streets toward the hospital, pushing speed limits and barely making stops.

When we hit the waiting room, Riggs makes a beeline for his woman, Luna, who is holding their daughter. The small space is filled wall to wall with family and friends. At that exact moment, Wick steps in, wearing a massive grin.

"I have a son," he announces, his voice thick with emotion.

The room erupts, cheers reverberating off the walls. I lean back against the cool wooden door frame, letting the moment's sheer energy wash over me as Wick's parents and Tequila's dad are the first to rush forward, their faces radiating pride and joy that lights up the entire space. One by one, friends and family step forward, their voices merging into a blend of congratulations, laughter, and excited chatter.

I stroll over to Wick. "Congratulations, brother." Gripping his shoulder tightly, I ask, "How's Tequila?"

Wick grins. "Good." His eyes sparkle with mischief. "She's insisting on seeing the family." He scans the room, relishing the moment and the love surrounding him.

Kiwi laughs. "Are they aware of how many of us there are?"

"Don't care. I'm just followin' orders, brother," Wick says, leading the way down the hall with one hell of a following in tow.

We pack into the small hospital room like a can of sardines, pumped to see Tequila and the newest Kings of Retribution family member. Wick sits on the edge of the bed, wrapping his arm around his woman, and the other hand resting on the tiny bundle wrapped in a soft blue blanket cradled in Tequila's arms. "Everyone," Wick says, and the room falls silent. He looks back down at his son. "I'd like you to meet Damien Dawson."

From where I stand, my gaze drifts across the room to where London stands next to Promise and Nova. Something stirs deep within me. It feels like a wave that rises from the pit of my stomach.

Thoughts of someday having a family of my own spiral through my mind.

Thoughts I don't need to feel while staring at London.

2

LONDON

For me, sitting in a courtroom is like a drug. I'm addicted to watching little bitches like Mitch Reeves sweat. Reeves is just as slimy as the client sitting to his right. Both men wear matching expressions of victory. The smug victory smirk is my favorite. I live for it. It makes grabbing imbeciles like Reeves and his client, Bradford Davis, by their balls so satisfying.

To recap, Mr. Davis blindsided his wife of thirty-five years with divorce papers six months ago. He tried to take the quick and easy route by claiming irreconcilable differences. At first, Mrs. Davis was going to accept it even though she was utterly devastated. But when Mr. Davis also announced he was leaving her with nothing but her personal items and the car he bought her five years ago, she decided it was time to fight.

I still remember the day Caroline Davis walked into my office. She was a wreck and lost. Mrs. Davis spent over thirty years dependent on her husband and was suddenly facing homelessness. *Not on my watch.* If I know anything, it's if a loving and devoted husband of thirty-plus years turns cold and distant out of the blue, you can bet your ass he's dipping his funky wick where it doesn't belong. Men are dogs, and they're all predictable. At first, Mrs. Davis insisted her husband would never cheat, but after some convincing, she finally agreed to let me hire a private detective to see what her not-so-loyal husband had been up to. I wasn't surprised to find out I was right.

Mrs. Davis, on the other hand, was devastated. I watched that poor woman's heart break. Then, she turned it into anger and rage. Rage, I could work with. It meant nailing her cheating husband's ass to the wall. Which is exactly what I'm about to do.

Yesterday, we sat and listened to Reeves' lame attempt at painting Mr. Davis as a picture-perfect husband. Today, however, is my time to shine. As Mr. Davis makes his way to the stand, I cut my eyes over to Reeves. He flashes me a killer smile—one that he thinks can bring any woman to her knees, when it would have me covering my drink.

Ignoring Reeves, I uncross my legs and stand. With my eye on the prize, I casually stand in front of the judge and Mr. Davis. "Mr. Davis, per your testimony yesterday, you'd consider yourself a good husband and provider, wouldn't you?"

Mr. Davis plasters on a fake smile. "Yes, I would say that's correct. I've always prided myself on being a devoted husband and father."

I nod. "And what about Mrs. Davis? Would you say she has been a good wife?"

Mr. Davis shrugs and the gesture pisses me off, but I keep my composure. Men like Mr. Davis see no real value in what it takes to be a homemaker.

"I guess so," he replies.

"You guess so?" I ask. "Wouldn't you think dropping out of college so she could get a job and support you while you finished medical school would constitute a good wife, Mr. Davis?"

"Yes, but—" Mr. Davis tries to cut in, but I don't give him the chance.

"Not only did Mrs. Davis give up her dreams of finishing medical school, but she also picked up a second job during your first year of residency to support the son you two had together?"

"Well..."

"Do you also recall promising your wife that you'd support her returning to school once you finished your residency?"

"I did, but—"

"Only you didn't follow through on that promise, did you, Mr. Davis? You decided you wanted to open your own practice. Therefore, your wife once again had to put her dreams on hold. But instead of going back to school, she continued to support you like a good wife while you built a successful practice. One that has been operating for over fifteen years."

Mr. Davis's face turns red with anger. "She could have gone back to school at any time."

"Is that right? Let's see, Mr. Davis. While you were finishing medical school and building your practice, your wife was busy working a full-time job, and when she was finally able to quit her job, she was busy raising your three children. What do you think a stay-at-home mom does all day, Mr. Davis?" I don't give him a chance to answer. "I'll tell you what a stay-at-home mom is. She is a maid, a nurse, a chauffeur, a teacher, a cook, a secretary, a mediator, a party planner, and a therapist. Being a stay-at-home mom is the single hardest job anyone is tasked with. Your wife dedicated thirty-five years to helping you build your dream while taking care of your family, and I find it rather insulting that when I asked you if Mrs. Davis was a good wife, you simply shrugged your shoulders. It seems to me, Mr. Davis, that you would not be where you are today if you did not have your wife. We also find it insulting that the only possessions you feel she is entitled to today are the car and the clothes on her back."

"Your honor." Reeves stands, cutting off my line of questioning.

Judge Bishop holds his hand up. "I'd like Mr. Davis to answer the question."

I nod my appreciation and turn back to Mr. Davis, who shifts uncomfortably in his chair. "I worked hard for my career."

"That wasn't what I asked, Mr. Davis. Would you or would you not be where you are today without your wife?"

Mr. Davis purses his lips. "No, but—"

"I didn't think so. Now, I'm going to move on to my next question. You stated yesterday that you simply fell out of love with your wife and that it wouldn't be fair to you or her to stay in a loveless marriage. Is that correct?"

"Yes, that's what I said."

"Hmm." I turn, walk over to the table where Mrs. Davis is sitting, and pick up a file folder. "So, you're saying it's not because you have been carrying on an affair with your partner's wife for the past ten months?"

Reeves flies to his feet once again. "Objection!"

"I have evidence, your honor." I hold up the folder.

"Overruled. You may proceed, Ms. Monroe."

"Thank you, your honor." I open the folder, producing the first photograph. "Mr. Davis, is this you in the photograph?" I hold up the image before him and watch as the color drains from his face.

"Ye... yes."

Approaching the bench, I hand over the image to the judge. "Your honor, as you can see, this is an image of Mr. Davis with his arms around and kissing a woman who is *not* his wife. I also want to note the time stamp on that photograph. It was taken just two days after Mr. Davis served Mrs. Davis with divorce papers. I have over sixty other photos of Mr. Davis and that same woman who has been identified as Melody Bartel, wife of Jim Bartel, Mr. Davis's partner." I hand over the folder to the judge. "I'd like to note, your honor, that my client is not only asking for half of all marital assets, but we are requesting compensation for emotional distress."

"Like hell!" Mr. Davis jumps to his feet. "She's not getting anywhere near my money." Spittle flies from his mouth.

Judge Bishop slams his gavel. "Mr. Davis, I'm going to suggest you keep your composure while in my courtroom." Judge Bishop then addresses Reeves. "Mr. Reeves, I'm advising you to keep your client in check. Another outburst like that and he will spend the night in jail."

"Yes, your honor," Reeves says, clearly agitated. "My apologies."

"Apologies! Those bitches are trying to rob me blind, and you're apologizing?"

I hide my smirk as the judge slams his gavel. "That is enough, Mr. Davis. I'm holding you in contempt."

"Your honor, if I may—" Reeves attempts to placate the judge but doesn't succeed.

"Save it, Mr. Reeves. I've heard all I need to hear and am ready to rule."

Reeves tries to argue once again. "But your honor, I haven't had time to investigate this so-called evidence my opposing counsel submitted before the court."

"Mr. Reeves, don't push your luck." Judge Bishop narrows his gaze. Lucky for Reeves, he still has some sense left and zips his lips.

"I hereby award Mrs. Davis half of the marital assets along with the house in which she and Mr. Davis shared. I'm also granting alimony in the sum of ten thousand dollars per month. Mr. Davis will also be required to pay Mrs. Davis the sum of five hundred and fifty thousand dollars in emotional distress damages, along with all of Mrs. Davis's attorney fees. The court is adjourned. Bailiff, please take Mr. Davis into custody, where he will spend the next twenty-four hours thinking about how he will behave in my courtroom." With his ruling made, Judge Bishop slams the gavel.

I turn to Mrs. Davis, who has a death grip on my hand and a look of disbelief on her face. "Did that just happen?"

"You bet your ass that just happened." I beam.

As if the weight of the world suddenly falls from her shoulders, Mrs. Davis looks at me with tears running down her face, then wraps her arms around me. I immediately return her embrace. This right here is why I do what I do. This incredibly kind and beautiful woman gave up her entire life for a man who in the end, had no appreciation and treated her like shit.

"I don't know what I can do to repay you for all you have done for me."

I look Mrs. Davis in the eyes. "Do you want to know how you can repay me?"

She nods.

"Go live your life for you. Go back to school. Go on that vacation you've always wanted. The world is at your fingertips."

"You're right." Mrs. Davis wipes the tears from her eyes. "I've been begging Bradford for years to take me to Australia. I think it's time I take myself."

"Hell yeah. And while you are down under, you should find yourself a hot Aussie who likes to go down under." I wink, making Mrs. Davis blush.

After we say our goodbyes, and I collect my belongings and head to the car, thirty minutes later, I arrive at my office. Promise greets me from her desk. "So, how was court? Did you make any grown men cry today?"

I plop down in the chair across from her desk. "Sadly, no. But I did cause one to throw a temper tantrum, which resulted in him losing half his assets, his house, being forced to pay alimony, and the pleasure of spending the night in jail," I relay while assessing the chipped polish on my nails, reminding me I'm in desperate need of a manicure.

"Damn, Lon, you're brutal." Promise giggles.

"I do try," I say, batting my lashes.

"On that note." Promise shakes her head. "How about lunch with your best friend to celebrate your victory?"

I sigh. "I'll have to take a rain check. Mom's facility called this morning and needs me to stop by."

Promise's face softens. "Is everything all right?"

I wave her off. "Yeah, yeah. They just have some paperwork for me to fill out. No biggie. Plus, her nurse said today was a good day, so I should stop in for a visit."

"Want me to come with you? I don't mind."

This is why I love my best friend. She's my rock. Promise and I met years ago while attending law school, and we have been inseparable since then. We have been by each other's sides through the many ups and downs in recent years. I was by her side when she made the horrible mistake of getting engaged to the world's biggest asshole, and I was there cheering her on when she finally got rid of him after she caught him cheating with her stepsister. Then, I was by her side when she met her now husband, Nova. Nova is the Enforcer for the Kings of Retribution. If you'd asked me a few years ago if my best friend would tie herself to an actual motorcycle club, I'd say you were out of your damn mind. Yet here we are. She's blissfully happy and in love. The two have the most adorable little boy, and Promise gained a stepdaughter, Piper, who is all kinds of sassy and amazing.

"Okay. If you're sure you don't need me, I'll just stop by the clubhouse and have lunch with Cain and Jaxson."

"I'm sure." I smile at Promise as she walks out of the office. "And give my Godson a kiss for me."

Pulling into the lot of my mom's living facility, I park and turn the car off. Tilting my head back against the headrest, I close my eyes, take a deep breath, and mentally prepare myself for a visit with my mother. Three years ago, at the age of fifty-eight, Mom was diagnosed with early-onset Alzheimer's. Though the diagnosis had been devastating, I was not expecting her to decline so rapidly. When she was first diagnosed, we talked about her coming to live with me, but being the fierce, unrepentant woman she is, she was adamantly against the idea. I understood the decision and respected it, but when Mom started forgetting her doctor's appointments, I was forced to put my foot down.

She still refused to live with me, but she did agree to have a nurse come sit with her a few hours a day. I always made sure to be there for her as well whenever I wasn't working. Then, last year, I was in the middle of court when I received a text from my mom's nurse. She had found Mom wandering down the street, and when she approached, Mom was disoriented and didn't seem to know where she was. That was the day I hired a full-time nurse. Susan stayed with Mom during the day, and I temporarily moved into Mom's house. Something anyone with a loved one with Alzheimer's is never prepared for is how rapidly the disease claims every aspect of their lives. I tried so hard to give my mother the care she needed and deserved, but I soon realized I was ill-equipped. I thank God every day for Susan. She helped me realize the decision to put my mom in a facility was what was best. Logically, I knew Susan was right. It's just my heart was telling me something different.

Most days, I felt like I was failing my mother. I wanted her to be safe and comfortable, but I also wanted her to live with dignity. This is why I researched and found the best facilities specializing in patients with advanced Alzheimer's disease. Unfortunately, this facility comes at a hefty price, even with mom's shitty insurance.

Which brings me back to why they called me here today. I'm a week late on this month's payment. It took all my savings to cover the first two months Mom was here. And though I make good money at my job, it's not enough to cover the bill and take care of my personal debts, along with a car loan, and other expenses it takes to help run a successful lawfirm. Six weeks ago, I made the decision to get a second job. To top it all off, I haven't told Promise. The secrecy is killing me, but I'm too ashamed to tell my own best friend that I'm drowning. Because I know if I told her, she'd insist on helping me, and I can't let her do that. Promise has her own family to think about. Not only that, but I also don't want anyone to know what I do every night.

Opening my eyes, I shake my head. "Pity party is over, London."

When I walk into the facility, I make my way to the director's office.

The receptionist greets me with a kind smile. "Can I help you?"

"I'm here to see Roger Briggs. He's expecting me. My name is London Monroe.

"Yes, ma'am. He said to send you in when you arrive." The receptionist gestures toward the open door to her left."

Mr. Briggs looks up from his computer and stands as I walk into his office. I take his offered hand.

"Thanks for agreeing to speak with me, Ms. Monroe. How are you doing today?" He motions for me to take a seat.

"I'm doing okay. Thank you."

As soon as Mr. Briggs takes a seat, he gets down to business. "I called you down today to discuss your mother's outstanding balance for the month."

"Yes. I just want to say how sorry I am for being late with the payment. I'm ready to settle that bill today." I reach into my purse and pull out a white envelope stuffed with cash. "It won't happen again."

Mr. Briggs takes the envelope offered, and I'm relieved he does so without judgment. "It's not a problem, Ms. Monroe."

My shoulders sag with relief. "Thank you and your staff for being kind to my mother. Knowing she's in such good hands helps me sleep a little better at night."

"It's our pleasure, Ms. Monroe."

I stand, and Mr. Briggs follows suit. "How is she today? I spoke with her nurse this morning, and she said today was a good day."

Mr. Briggs smiles. "Indeed, it is. I checked on your mother about an hour ago, and she was in good spirits. I'll walk you down to see her. Today, we had some students from the hair academy visit. One of the young ladies gave your mom a wash and curl. And she's looking forward to chair yoga later this afternoon."

"That sounds wonderful." I beam as Mr. Briggs leads me into the rec room, where I spot my mom sitting by a window, chatting with one of the other residents. The second her eyes land on me, her face lights up. Nothing in this world can bring out the little girl butterflies in me like when my mom looks at me like I'm her whole world. Growing up, I never had any doubt about how special I was to my mom because she not only showed me but also told me every day how much she loved me.

"Doodlebug." She reaches for me, and I waste no time falling into her embrace.

"Hey, Momma." I close my eyes and breathe in the familiar scent of her perfume.

"I didn't know you were coming to see me today," she says.

"Well, I finished with court and thought I'd come to see my favorite person."

"Oh yeah." Mom gets that sassy glint in her eye. "You kick some ass today?"

I throw my head back and laugh. "You know it, Momma."

3

EVEREST

The first bit of morning light creeps through the thin-ass curtains, casting just enough glow to piss me off. I grunt, my body stiff as hell, every muscle reminding me of what I've put my body through over the past few days. My arms feel like lead, and my ribs ache like they've been used for batting practice, accompanied by bone-deep exhaustion different from what I've experienced before.

The thing is, I had no damn business being there. No real training, no experience. Not like everyone else. All I had was the need to prove to Riggs and myself that I could do the job. And I did. I feel like shit, but it was all worth it. I got to do something that mattered and send a few low-life motherfuckers to their graves in the process.

With a heavy breath, I swing my legs over the edge of the bed, planting my feet on the cool wooden floor. I roll my shoulder, trying to release the tension, then push up to stand and drag my ass across the room toward the bathroom.

I keep the light off and reach behind the shower curtain, turning the shower knob. After a moment, steam fills the room, getting hot and thick. I yank off my boxers and step into the tub, allowing the scalding water to hit my skin, then brace my hands against the cold, hard tiles as the heat rolls over me. It digs deep into my muscles, soothing my shoulders and back. The water pounds down, loosening the tightness in my muscles. I shut my eyes, savoring the sensation, letting the exhaustion fade.

After the hot shower turns cold, I shut off the water and reach for a towel. Heat rolls off me in waves, clinging to my skin as I wipe the steam from the mirror. I look at my reflection and study my face. For a second, it's not just me looking back, but my old man's eyes, his square jaw, the set of his mouth when he's working through something, and it's all there, staring me down. I immediately think of home and my folks back in Minnesota.

I run a hand over my face, dragging it down my neck. Some men are built for peace, for a quiet life. Like my father. But not me. I need the adrenaline, the purpose, the fight. That's why I had to leave Minnesota years ago.

I walk out of the bathroom, drag on a pair of worn jeans, the denim soft against my skin, and pull a black tee over my head, the fabric stretching tight across my chest and shoulders.

I stroll barefoot into the kitchen, the old floorboards groaning under my weight as I prepare my coffee. The rich, earthy aroma fills the air as it brews, the dark water dripping into the pot. Once ready, I pour myself a mug.

The early morning air greets me when I step out onto the balcony. It mingles the scents of freshly baked bread from nearby bakeries and the distant brine of the Mississippi River, along with the stench of stale beer and cigarette smoke clinging to the damp air. I take a sip of coffee, the bold, slightly bitter taste grounding me as I scan the street below.

Bourbon Street is never quiet, not even at this hour. A few stragglers from last night weave along the sidewalks, their steps unsteady, voices low and sluggish. Street cleaners move down the block with hoses, washing away the grime. Across the street, a couple of bartenders lean against a doorway, smoking. Neon signs still flicker, their glow paling against the creeping daylight.

The city is waking up, but it never really sleeps. The scent of strong chicory coffee drifts from a nearby café. A delivery truck rumbles past, its tires splashing through puddles left behind by the street cleaners. A beat of silence passes, but it's not long before the low buzz of conversations starts as early risers and workers add to the city's rhythm. New Orleans is always alive and pulsing with a constant undercurrent that never stops.

Living above Twisted Throttle has its perks. It makes working at the bar downstairs convenient. Riggs and his old lady, Luna, lived here before expanding their family. Now, it's my sanctuary.

I take another sip and reflect on the journey that brought me here. Growing up in a small Minnesota town, my world revolved around hockey. As an only child, I poured everything into the sport, dreaming of going pro one day. I carried those hopes and dreams through high school and into college. Unfortunately, a series of events sidetracked those plans. During a college game, a brutal hit twisted my knee into an unnatural position. The pain was instant and blinding—the diagnosis, a torn ACL and MCL.

Rehab was grueling, but I pushed through it, fighting like hell to keep my dreams alive. I told myself I'd return stronger than before, so I made every hour in the gym, every excruciating step count.

Aside from being benched from playing the sport I loved, I also hadn't ridden in months. The Harley I'd built from the frame up sat in the garage untouched. Riding was my therapy. The road was a place where I found clarity and freedom, and I needed it. I was itching to feel the wind on my face and the vibration of my bike beneath me. When I was strong enough to ride again, I didn't hesitate.

I'm jolted back to that day and the moment that ultimately altered my future for good.

The sharp curve I took too fast.

The moment I realized the tires weren't gripping the asphalt.

The gut-wrenching weightlessness as my body launched from the bike.

The brutal impact that rattled my bones and tore my flesh.

The taste of blood in my mouth.

The fire in my ribs as I gasped for air as I lay broken on the side of the road, my bike a twisted wreck beside me.

Just like that, everything I'd worked for and the dream I'd built my life around were gone.

I was back at square one.

I spent months in rehab and was told I could never perform at the level needed to continue playing hockey. I became a shadow of myself, drowning my bitterness, hate, and frustration in alcohol. The bottle numbed the weight pressing against my chest but never lifted it. I drank until the fire in my gut turned to ice, and the rage inside me felt distant. But it never really disappeared. It just waited, hungry and ready to strike. Eventually, whiskey wasn't enough to keep my inner turmoil at bay. That's when I became heavily involved with underground fight clubs. The rush I got from bare-knuckle brawls became my drug of choice.

Underground fighting was different. It didn't just dull the anger, it unleashed it. The moment I stepped into that ring, the world outside faded. The deafening roar of the crowd, the sweat, and the metallic tang of blood in the air fed the chaos inside.

Every brutal blow my opponent landed made me feel alive. The pain was a welcome distraction. I'd strike back, my knuckles splitting, flesh and bones crushing beneath my fists. The rush was intoxicating, a primal high that drowned out everything. I lost myself in the raw, unfiltered violence of the fight.

It was more than winning.

It was about control.

And I didn't stop when I should've, pushing past limits, past reason and mercy until one night I went too far.

I don't remember what made me snap and shut off all reason. Maybe the guy talked too much shit or hit me wrong. Perhaps it was too many nights with too much whiskey in my veins and rage clawing at my insides. All I know is my fists kept swinging long after they should have stopped, followed by muffled yelling being drowned out by the roaring in my ears. Tunnel vision slowed everything down except for my knuckles hitting his flesh.

When I finally came back to myself, the guy was on the ground, not moving, and his chest rose in shallow, uneven breaths, his face bloody and swollen. And for the first time, as I stared down at him, the rush didn't drown out the weight pressing on my chest. It made it heavier.

That was my wake-up call.

I wasn't in control.

I wasn't coping.

I was self-destructing.

I inhale sharply, my grip tightening around the mug in my hand. The pain of that moment lingers, not just in my body but deep in my fucking soul. The resentment, the anger at the life I lost, it simmers under my skin for a few seconds.

Then, I shake it off.

That's not my life anymore.

I've made peace with it.

I had to.

After that incident, my eyes were wide open. I needed a change. I was desperate for it. So, I stood in my room, staring at a map on the wall. I needed a new purpose, a fresh start in life, and it needed to be anywhere but Minnesota. I closed my eyes and threw a dart. It landed on New Orleans—a city rich with culture, music, and a promise of rebirth—so I packed what I could carry, hugged my folks, and left my hometown, seeking redemption in the Crescent City.

This is where I discovered the Kings. The brotherhood within the club filled a significant void in my life. Being part of the MC gave me a sense of purpose and belonging that I needed. Riggs and the others allowed me to be a part of something bigger than myself.

This life isn't something that everyone can endure. It's a path carved from the trials and tribulations we face daily. In this world, death hides in the corners while we claw for a taste of redemption. It's a life I've chosen, bled for, and thrive on.

I down the rest of my coffee and don't dwell on a past that is dead.

I let myself get stuck once.

And I won't do it again.

***

The bar is packed tonight. A thick haze of smoke hangs in the air, along with the scent of whiskey and the ever-present musk of Bourbon Street. The deep thrum of Fender's guitar growls through the speakers, his voice rough as sandpaper as he belts out an old rock classic. Like always, the crowd, especially the women, are eating it up with drinks raised, their bodies moving, and voices shouting along in drunken celebration.

I stand near the door, arms crossed, eyes scanning the room. Tonight, like most nights, I'm security. My presence alone is enough to keep most people in check, but there's always some asshole looking to test his luck.

A couple of tourists stumble past me, one of them eyeing my cut with a mix of curiosity and caution. It's easy to spot the outsiders. Tourists move differently, always looking around like they expect the city to bite. Locals walk with purpose. They know which streets to avoid and where to find the best damn authentic Louisiana cuisine.

The heat inside is pressing against me, so I look across the room, locking eyes with Catcher, who is helping with crowd control tonight, and give him a chin lift, letting him know I'm stepping out for a minute. I step into the thick Louisiana air, lean against the brick wall, pull a cigarette from my pack, and light up. The first drag hits my lungs and as I glance around, the street outside is alive with neon lights and revelers, some on unsteady legs, with drinks in hand. I exhale, watching the smoke curl into the night.

Kiwi steps out, exhaling like he just walked off the battlefield. "The place is packed, and all the family is here tonight." He rolls his shoulders. "Our women are inside raisin' hell." He takes a pull from his beer, then side-eyes me. "Except for London. She's MIA."

I take a long drag of my cigarette and flick the ash onto the pavement, keeping my face neutral, though my interest is piqued. One thing about London is that she likes to have a good time and never misses a night out with the women. But this is the third time she's skipped out on them in the past few weeks. I glance at Kiwi, and he's grinning like the Cheshire cat.

"Maybe she's on a date with some suit and tie," Kiwi quips, trying to get a rise out of me.

"Not her type," I fire back, and Kiwi chuckles. Before he can continue to poke me, a tall woman with long blonde hair struts right up to me with a confident air that screams she's used to getting what she wants.

"You got a name, big guy?" she purrs, running a red-painted nail down my tattooed arm.

Kiwi snorts, taking a sip of his beer as he watches.

I should be interested. Hell, a few months ago, I would have been. I wouldn't have hesitated in taking her to my bed, burying myself in her, and letting it be nothing more than a way to take the edge off. But that was before London got under my goddamn skin. No matter how many women I have in my bed, it's London I want. It's her sharp tongue, her fucking fire, the way she looks at me like she's daring me to make a move. It's a fucking distraction I don't want but can't shake. And it's pissing me off more than I care to admit.

The woman before me shifts, stepping close, waiting for an answer.

I take another drag and exhale. I gotta give it to her, she's bold as fuck, but I'm not biting. "Not interested."

She tilts her head, pouting. "You sure about that?" She presses her large fake tits against my abdomen. I've got easy pussy ripe for the taking, and my dick isn't interested because everything about this woman is not what I crave.

I grin, slow and easy. "Pretty sure."

She shrugs. "Your loss, big guy." She takes the rejection and walks back to the group of women she was with.

Beside me, Kiwi damn near chokes on his drink, more for theatrics than anything. Luckily, he keeps his trap shut.

I push off the wall and head back inside. The loud bass slams into my chest as Fender starts another set, and the energy in the bar amplifies.

Then, I see him, a wiry, greasy-looking fucker in a leather jacket lingering around a back corner table, his hands moving in a way I've seen a thousand times before. A quick trade and a few bills are exchanged.

The son of a bitch is selling drugs.

Not on my watch.

My eyes follow the stupid son of a bitch as he slips away, disappearing into the bathroom.

I move with a purpose across the room. On my way, I pass the bar where Catcher is posted, and next to him is Nova, with his woman, Promise, tucked close to him. Catcher clocks me immediately but doesn't speak.

"Got a situation," I tell him, keeping my voice low. He nods once. I don't wait for him to follow and keep heading toward the back of the bar.

Inside the bathroom, the stench of piss and cheap cologne punches me in the face. Over by the sinks, a couple of guys linger, talking shit about a Saints game.

"Out," I bark, and they quickly exit.

The dealer is at the urinal, his back to me, pissing. I step up behind him, close enough to make him feel my presence.

"Fuck off trying to catch a look at my dick, you sick bastard," he mutters while zipping up.

I grab the back of his head and slam it into the wall. He grunts, stumbling back.

"The fuck?" He scrambles to regain his balance.

"You're sellin' shit in the wrong bar, motherfucker." My tone is low and dangerous.

The bastard's lip curls as he sizes me up. "What the fuck you gonna do about it?"

I don't answer. I let my fists do the talking. My first punch connects with his gut, folding him like a lawn chair. He wheezes, staggering back, but he quickly recovers, reaching into his jacket and flicking a knife open.

I smirk. The little fucker has some fight in him. I like that.

"I'm gonna teach you not even a big son of a bitch like you is untouchable," he sneers, quickly lunging at me. The tip of his blade nicks my forearm. The motherfucker is fast, I'll give him that. But I'm quicker. I grab his wrist and twist hard, and the blade clatters to the floor. Unarming him isn't enough for me. I apply more pressure until his bones snap. His scream echoes through the bathroom as I continue to inflict pain, driving my fist into his ribs a few times, knocking the air from his lungs.

Then I reach into his jacket pocket, pulling out a bag of pills. Without a second thought, I toss them in the urinal, watching them dissolve in the filth.

"You stupid motherfucker," the dealer spits, clutching his ribs, his voice thick with pain and rage. "You don't know who you're fucking with."

I grip him by the collar of his jacket and pull him toward the bathroom door, his boots sliding against the tile floor. Catcher is standing just outside as I step out.

"Need a hand?" he asks, raising an eyebrow while eyeing the dealer's broken wrist.

I keep my grip firm and steady. "Under control, brother." I push past him.

Heads turn as I shove past bodies and tables across the room, hauling the punk toward the door to throw his ass out.

Riggs stands near the entrance with Nova. He scans the guy, then narrows his eyes at me. "Explain."

"Peddlin' pills in the bar," I reply, and Riggs' expression hardens. He steps in close, towering over the dealer. "You got two choices, motherfucker. Disappear, or I make you disappear." His voice is lethal.

After Riggs' threat, I toss the bastard out onto the street.

He lands hard, and tourists step around him, knowing better than to get involved. He looks at me, chest heaving and eyes wild. "This ain't over," he grits.

I stand over him, my stare pressing him into the concrete. My voice is calm but deadly. "It's over. You show your face again, they'll either be draggin' the river for you, or they'll find your corpse floatin' in the bayou."

His eyes narrow at my threat, but he says nothing. Instead, he gets to his feet and disappears into the crowd.

I take out another cigarette, flick my lighter, and pull in a slow drag, exhaling a plume of smoke—just another night at Twisted

Throttle. But as I watch the smoke curl, my jaw tightens. The drug problem in this city is getting worse, with dealers slithering in like snakes, poisoning our streets.

This is our city.

Our turf.

And I'll be damned if we let it rot under our watch.

4

LONDON

I'm getting ready for work when my cell phone rings. Promise's name lights up the screen. I answer, placing the call on speaker to finish applying my eyeshadow. "What's up?"

"I'm calling in for an impromptu girls' night. Cain is on munchkin duty, and I desperately need a cosmo and a conversation that doesn't involve potty training or motorcycles. I already talked to Sadie and Ruby, and they're in."

Fuck. I hate lying to my best friend. "I'm sorry, Promise, but I can't make it."

"What? Why? You bailed on us last time, Lon."

God, I feel like a shit friend. "I know, and I'm sorry. It's just, today drained me."

"How is your mom?" Promise's tone changes to one of concern.

I sigh. "Today was a challenge. I hate this, Promise. Two days ago, she was herself. Cracking jokes and asking me about work. Then, today, she was agitated and didn't remember who I was. Finally, I had to leave so the nurse could get her to settle down."

"Oh, Lon. I'm so sorry. I wish there was something I could do."

"Thanks, Promise. Just hearing you say that helps."

"I'll always be here for you, Lon. The club too. You're not alone."

I stare at my reflection in the mirror and watch as a single tear rolls down my cheek. I'm desperate to ask for help and lean on my friend, but my pride won't allow it. Not only did I inherit my sassy mouth from my mother, but I also got my strong sense of pride from her. Being raised by an incredibly strong, independent single mom will do that to you. Growing up, it was just Mom and me. My father bailed on his family when I was a baby, so I have no memory of him. In anger, Mom burned every picture of him after he left. When I was five, my kindergarten class was having a daddy-daughter party. That was the first time I asked my mom about my father. She explained things to me the best way she could. Mom also let me ditch school that day and instead took me to the strawberry festival. I may not have grown up with a dad, but I was never made to feel like I was missing out.

"Lon, are you still there?" Promise asks.

I shake my wandering thoughts away. "Yeah. I zoned out a minute there."

"I'm going to let you go so you can get some rest then. I'll talk to Ruby and Sadie about rescheduling girls' night."

"Don't do that," I tell her. "You should go out and have some fun."

"Yeah, maybe. Or I could ask Piper if she wants to catch a movie. You get some rest, and I'll see you at the office on Monday. Or if you need me before, call, okay."

"I will. Thanks, Promise."

"Anytime, babe."

I end the call with Promise and note that I only have thirty minutes to be at work. I'll just have to finish my hair and makeup there. Walking into my closet, I slip my sneakers on and grab my duffle bag. When I walk out of my apartment, I'm relieved to not see the creepy dude who lives across from me. I've been living in the same complex for a few years now, and although it's not in a great part of town, I've never really had any trouble with it aside from my neighbor. He doesn't do anything per se, he just makes it a point to let his beady little eyeballs linger where they shouldn't. The dude makes my skin crawl.

I can't help letting my thoughts drift back in time on the drive to work, thinking about how unfair life has been for my mom. She deserved so much better than life has given her. I once asked her why she named me London. She said she's always dreamed of traveling, and London was number one on her bucket list. For years, I swore I'd take my mom on that dream vacation. That day never came, and now it's too late. I blame myself, too. I kept putting it off, thinking we had more time. My mother spent her entire life devoted to me, giving me everything and even working two jobs to send me to college so I could achieve my dream of becoming a lawyer. *But what about her dreams?*

Before I know it, I'm pulling up in front of Pink Paradise. The club is located twenty-five miles outside of New Orleans. I chose this club because I have slim chances of running into anyone I know.

"Hey, London, Tony is looking for you," Journey tells me the second I breeze through the back door.

"Tell him to keep his pants on. I'll be there in a minute." I go to the dressing room and throw my bag in my locker. Behind me, Kimmy struts in, wearing a hot pink thong and head-to-toe body glitter. She has a massive smile on her face. That can only mean one thing. "Good night?"

"You know it. You should get your cute ass out there while the getting is good."

"I am. I'm going to see what Tony wants first."

I exit the dressing room, walk down to the end of the hall to Tony's office, and find him sitting behind his desk. Tony is an older man, and if I had to guess, I would say he's pushing sixty. He stands at least six feet tall, has broad shoulders, and is a little bit of a gut, but otherwise is in good shape. He keeps his gray hair back in a ponytail and wears god-awful eighties windbreaker tracksuits daily. Tony runs his club with an iron fist and doesn't stand for any bullshit. He also respects and protects his girls.

I knock on his door. "Hey, Tony. Journey said you wanted to see me?"

Tony looks up from the stack of invoices on his desk. "Hiya, darlin'. Come in and have a seat."

"Everything okay?' I ask, sitting in the chair across from him.

"There's somethin' I wanted to discuss with you."

"Okay," I say, confused.

"Listen." Tony rubs the back of his neck. "Under normal circumstances, I wouldn't come to you with this shit. I respect that you want to keep this part of your life private, considering what you do for a living. You have your reason, and I'd never say shit to a soul."

Another thing about Tony is that he knows everything about everyone who steps foot into his club. I don't know how or where he gets his information, and I've never asked. All I know is he knows who I am, what I do for a living, where I live, and he knows about my mom. And it might sound crazy because I've only known Tony for less than two months, but I trust him. I've seen firsthand how he cares about his girls and all his employees. When I say he looks out for everyone here, I mean it.

"I know you wouldn't, Tony. I appreciate that. Really."

"I got your back, sweetheart. Which is why I wouldn't be askin' this of you if I had another choice."

"Ask me what?"

Tony runs his hand over the top of his head. "Amara has gotten herself in some trouble with that new fella."

Suddenly, I'm on alert. Amara is one of the dancers here. She's twenty-two and the sweetest girl—way too sweet and shy for this place. Everyone here, especially Tony, looks out for her. "What about her? Is she okay?"

Tony shakes his head. "Showed up tonight with a black eye, busted lip, and a sprained wrist. She tried to hide it under makeup, but the bruises were clear as day."

My hands ball into fists. "Was it that son of a bitch boyfriend of hers?"

Tony's face turns hard. "After some coaxing, she admitted it was. I wanted to go after the son of a bitch myself, but you know Amara, she got scared."

"That bastard can't get away with putting his hands on her," I fume.

"I agree. I had Journey take her to the hospital, and she was able to talk Amara into pressing charges. Amara said this dude has money and connections. She's terrified. I'm not sure if that's true or if the fucker has been blowin' smoke up her ass to make her think he's somebody. I'm on the case and gonna find out what I can."

"What do you need from me?" I ask.

"If Amara is willing to go the distance, I want to hire you as her lawyer. It's not really my style to go by the books, but this is the hand I'm playing for now. If I look into this guy and shit looks too dangerous, I'll pull you back. I'm asking you because Amara will trust you. Also, because I know your reputation."

I smirk. "My reputation?"

Tony leans back in his chair. "Don't you make grown men cry?"

I roll my eyes. "I guess I do have a reputation."

After talking with Tony, I head back to the dressing room to prepare for my set. I keep this part of my life separate from my everyday life. I know I shouldn't feel ashamed, but I do. I take my clothes off for money to care for my mother.

What would my mom think of me if she knew?

What would my friends think?

Unfortunately, I feel shame due to society's portrayal of women. The judgment should actually fall on everyone else. I mean, I look at Journey and see a single mom who works her ass off to take care of her two kids. Her youngest son has a disability, and she started working at the club two years ago to afford sending him to a private school. Then you have Kimmy, whose parents kicked her out when she turned eighteen. She didn't let her shitty parents stop her from making something of herself. She works at the club three nights a week to pay for her tuition. Those who genuinely know these women, the sacrifices they have made, and know their hearts could only sing praises. Nobody chooses dancing as their first option. I know I didn't. It was the only option where I could make enough to keep my mother in Golden Hills.

Who would have thought those pole dancing exercise classes I took back in college would be helpful? At first, Promise and I signed up for the classes on a dare. Back then, pole dancing was not as popular as it is now. Promise made it through three classes before ultimately deciding it wasn't for her. To be fair, my best friend is not very coordinated. However, I loved it. I kept at it, attending class at least three times a week for about two years. I gave it up when life got busy, and school kept me in the trenches. It turns out that all these years later, working the pole is like riding a bike.

I'm securing my wig when Lucas, one of the bouncers, walks by and raps his knuckles against the dressing room door. "You're up, London."

"Okay." I stand and give myself one last look in the floor-length mirror. The long, wavy red wig I wear to cover my natural black hair makes my amber eyes pop. The wig, coupled with the heavy makeup, makes me look like a different person, which was my main goal when I started working here.

"Knock 'em dead," Journey sings songs as I strut to the stage. This is the part of my night where I mentally turn off all emotion and block out the fact that dozens of eyes will be on my body. Each person in the crowd becomes a blur, a nameless face, a means to an end. I've gotten good at getting lost in the music and ignoring the shame and humiliation that comes with the job. I'd do anything to ensure my mother is taken care of. That includes taking my clothes off for strangers.

As soon as I climb the steps behind the stage, the DJ plays "Crazy Bitch" by Buckcherry. The room is dark, aside from the low hue of strobe lights illuminating the stage. Taking a deep breath, I plaster on a fake, seductive smile and slowly step onto the stage. With each exaggerated sway of my hips, I draw the attention of every red-blooded man in the room. Running my palms up my body and along my breasts, I confidently approach center stage. Once I reach the pole, I hold onto it with my right hand and circle it.

Closing my eyes, I get lost in the music. With my back to the audience, I hook my leg around the pole, completing my first spin before swiftly transitioning into my next move, where I face the pole and then, with both hands, pull myself up. I end my transition with a fireman slide. Once my knees hit the stage, I throw my body back, thrusting my breasts toward the ceiling. Next, I make a show of running my palms against my belly before slowly removing the tiny scrap of material covering my breasts. The ringing in my ears and my heart pounding drown out the catcalls and whistles.

5

EVEREST

The humid air is thick with the scent of rain from the night before while I ride through the city. As I roll up to Creole Café, I ease off the throttle, the smell of coffee and fried dough cutting through the air. Mrs. Maggie has been running this place longer than I've been alive, and she treats every one of us Kings like we're her blood. She's got a heart bigger than this whole damn city.

Parking out front, I swing my leg over and stroll inside, the little bell above the door jingling. The café is already busy with locals getting their morning fix. Mrs. Maggie clocks me the second I step in.

"Hey, baby." She smiles while pouring coffee for a customer.

"Mornin', Mrs. Maggie."

She reaches for a to-go box. "Want the usual?"

I smile, leaning against the counter. "Double order this time. Got work to do at the youth center, and Charlie ain't a man who turns down a good meal."

Mrs. Maggie laughs. "You're right about that." She starts putting together my order, moving with the practiced ease of someone feeding this city for decades. "Y'all are doin' good over there, Everest. The kids need strong men to show them the right path."

I nod and appreciate her praise, though that's not why I do it. "Just tryin' to give them somethin' solid, somewhere they belong."

She slides the two stuffed containers across the counter. "And that is why I'll always feed you for free, baby. Y'all are changing lives."

Like always, I press a few bills into the tip jar, earning a side-eye from her before grabbing the food boxes. "I appreciate you, Mrs. Maggie."

"Stay safe and give Charlie my best." She waves me off, already turning to greet another customer.

I head back outside, securing the food before firing up my bike again. The ride to the youth center is short. I roll up to the old building we've been working on. When we got our hands on it, it was falling apart.

I park near the side entrance, kill the engine, grab the food, and head inside. I glance around, taking in the new mats, heavy bags, the ring, and weights. The space still smells of fresh paint and sawdust.

The Kings threw in a good chunk of money for the gym. The rest of our funding came from private donors who still give a damn about the city's future. And it isn't just the money that matters. The time, effort, and hands-on work make a difference.

I don't do this for recognition. I do it because I know firsthand what it's like to need an outlet, a place to put your anger, energy, and pain. Too many kids don't have someone looking out for them. Some of them come from broken homes or the streets. Some need a safe place where they're not being judged or written off.

"Everest," a deep, weathered voice calls from the other side of the gym.

I see Charlie Ray Bradford approaching me, wiping his hands

on a rag. He's in his late sixties but still built like a brick wall despite his age, and his skin is dark and lined from years spent working under the Louisiana sun. Charlie has been a counselor in the community for decades. He's the kind of man who doesn't waste time on bullshit, just straight talk and hard lessons. He's got the respect of every kid who's ever walked through his doors, and he damn sure has mine.

"Brought breakfast," I say.

Charlie grins. "Now that's what I'm talkin' about." He rubs his belly.

I follow him to a couple of folding chairs near the boxing ring and set the food on a stack of gym mats. We pop open the containers, and steam rises from inside, carrying the aroma of butter, spice, and deep-fried perfection. Mrs. Maggie didn't skimp, not that she ever does. There's a generous portion of shrimp and grits. Next to it is a flaky buttermilk biscuit the size of my damn fist slathered in cane syrup and butter. And a breakfast from Maggie wouldn't be complete without a couple of fried pork chops sitting on top of a heaping pile of smothered potatoes and onions.

Charlie whistles as he grabs his biscuit. "Maggie outdone herself." He takes a bite.

I grin, tearing into the pork chops. "Wouldn't expect anything less."

Charlie chews for a moment. "This is the kind of meal that'll make a man rethink his life."

I chuckle, digging into some shrimp and grits.

Charlie gestures around the room. "This is all coming together. We should be able to open it to the community by next week."

I nod. "I can't wait. Too many kids out there needing an outlet to burn off what's eatin' them up inside."

"You're not wrong. Boxing saved my ass when I was young and kept me out of trouble most of the time. It gave me something to work toward. And that's what these kids need—discipline and structure. We can provide them with a fight they can win without ending up behind bars or dead," Charlie states.

And that's what this is all about. Some of these kids, who will walk through these doors, are one bad choice away from being swallowed by the streets. Gangs, drugs, violence, it's all out there waiting for the next victim. This gym and the boxing program are a chance to show them they don't have to end up another damn statistic.

"Have you ever stepped inside a ring?" Charlie asks.

I chuckle, wiping my mouth with a napkin. "Not like you did. My fights weren't exactly sanctioned."

Charlie grins. "Humor an old man. Let's see what you got."

I shake my head, but I'm already moving, following him to the ring. "You sure about this, old man?" I tease.

"I ain't dead yet."

Donning gloves, we step into the ring, tap fists, and move. We spar lightly, testing each other. Charlie throws a jab, and I block it, moving in close with a controlled hook that stops short of impact. His grin widens. "You got control. That's good." He steps back and rolls his shoulders. "You ever thought about training these kids yourself? I could use the help."

I exhale. "Not sure I'm right for the job."

Charlie stops moving and gives me a serious look. "You show up, put in the time, and set an example already. The kids respect you. Most of all, they believe in you because they can count on you. That's half the job done right there." Charlie claps me on the back, his voice laced with conviction. "You're already changing lives, Everest."

I reflect on the kids I've worked with over the years. Opening this gym is about breaking down barriers. We may not change everyone who walks through our doors, but if we can improve even one person's life, every effort and time is worthwhile.

I look at Charlie. "Count me in."

We let that end our impromptu sparring, roll up our sleeves, and finish the last bit of work in the gym.

Night settles on the city by the time we complete today's tasks, and finally, we can officially open the doors in a few days. And now, all I want to do is go home, sit on the couch with a beer and a cold slice of pizza from the refrigerator, and watch television. "I'm headin' out," I tell Charlie, who has his keys in hand.

"I appreciate the help today." He flicks the switch on the wall, and the overhead lights turn off.

I nod. "Anytime."

"The club coming to the grand opening?" Charlie asks.

"Wouldn't miss it." I walk toward the door, with Charlie following behind me. We step outside, and I wait while he locks the door.

"Stay safe," he says, then heads to his old beat-up truck.

"You too, old man." Then I wait for him to climb inside and drive away before heading to my bike.

I glance around the mostly quiet parking lot and notice Jace, a kid from the youth center who is barely eighteen, caught up in conversation with a couple of men between the building and a dumpster. The bastard on the left looks familiar. Beneath the dim glow of the streetlights, I see the bruises his face is sporting from the beating I gave him a few nights ago. But it's the cast on his arm that solidifies his identity.

This motherfucker has a death wish.

My blood turns hot, and my boots hit the pavement hard as I close the distance. "Yo, Jace."

The kid startles, his eyes wide like a deer caught in headlights. "Everest, I was just—"

"Go home," I cut him off, my tone sharp, but I keep my eyes on the drug pushers. "*Now.*" I bark at the kid. Jace doesn't argue. He mutters something under his breath, then takes off.

The second pusher, an ugly son of a bitch with a rat face,

watches Jace jog away and clicks his tongue. "That's a shame. The kid had potential." He then glares at me.

I stare the motherfucker down, knowing he's out here on the streets recruiting. "Yeah? So do graveyards." My attention shifts to the wiry prick I dealt with earlier in the week.

He steps forward, his busted lip sneering at me. "You should have minded your business."

I already see it coming, the shift in his buddy's stance and the slight hitch in his breath before the motherfucker reaches for his waistband. When his fingers brush the handle of his piece, mine is already aimed between his eyes.

He freezes, and his greasy friend stiffens beside him. I disarm the bastard, sliding his gun behind the waistband of my jeans for safekeeping.

"My boss knows about you." The prick from the other night at the bar smirks.

I laugh, but there's no humor in it. "That right?"

He swallows hard but keeps his mouth running while I keep my gun trained on his rat-faced friend. "He doesn't like you or your biker friends fucking with his operation." He looks me up and down. "So back the fuck off before something bad happens."

I contemplate whether I should pull the trigger and send my own message back to his boss in the form of a corpse, but quickly decide against it. For now. At least until the club discovers who has the brass balls to continue encroaching on Kings' territory. I smirk, but there's nothing friendly about it. "Run back to your boss and tell him the Kings don't take kindly to threats." I lean in, my voice dripping with something dark. "You tell him if he likes breathin' to pack his shit and get the fuck out of our city, or he'll be diggin' his own grave."

The muscles in the bastard's jaw tick, but he says nothing. They waste no time taking off, vanishing down the alley like sewer rats.

Suddenly, headlights flicker in the darkness, and a vehicle creeps cautiously toward me. My weapon stays poised at my side, my grip tight and ready. As the old truck finally halts, I lock eyes with Charlie through the windshield. The old man saw everything, stayed hidden, and had my back just in case. I holster my weapon as he leans over and rolls down the truck's window.

"I'll be right behind you," he says.

I nod, then stroll to my bike, swing my leg over the seat, and fire her up. My fingers tighten around the grip as I pull out of the parking lot, with Charlie falling behind me.

I get the feeling this isn't over.

Not by a long shot.

A short drive later and it's damn near midnight when my head hits the pillow. But my eyes instantly snap open at the sharp buzzing of my phone. I snatch it off the nightstand. It's Riggs. I answer, "Yeah," and rub my eyes.

"Catcher called. The trail camera near the river caught movement. Need you to get over there and back him up should there be trouble."

I'm already sitting up, swinging my legs over the side of the bed. "On it."

"Report back," Riggs orders, and then he kills the call.

My body runs on autopilot, and I move fast, slipping on jeans, a shirt, boots, and my cut. My gun is on the nightstand. I grab it, check the magazine, and slide it into my holster.

Once outside, the humid night air clings to my skin as I sling a leg over my bike, fire the engine, and roll out.

I kill the light and cut the engine about a block away from the clubhouse, and coast to a stop. The last thing I want is to announce myself should the trespasser still be lurking. In the distance, the clubhouse sits along the river. Next to it, the old mill looms in the darkness, abandoned for many years. Beyond that, the club's fence line runs toward the river. I pull my phone out and dial Catcher.

"Everest," he answers, his voice hoarse.

"I'm coming in from the west. Take the east. If someone's still out here, they'll have to hit the water."

"Copy."

I pocket the phone and pick up the pace, the gravel shifting under my boots. I take out my weapon, arming myself. The wind carries the smell of damp earth and rusting metal. Everything else around me is shadow and silence.

Then, I catch the scent of fresh cigarette smoke.

I slow my steps, scanning my surroundings. The shed looms ahead, a structure we use when problems need to be dealt with— the kind that gets dumped into the muddy Mississippi when we're done.

I see a cigarette butt, still burning, the ember glowing against the dirt as I get closer. I crouch, looking out at the water close by. The light of a few barges glows in the distance, but the water is too dark to see much else. No boat. There's no movement beyond the river's slow lapping against the bank. But someone was just here. Maybe they still are. Watching. Listening.

I hear boot steps creeping up behind me. I whip around, weapon ready. "Shit," I hiss, lowering my arm but keeping my eyes sharp on Catcher.

"Anything?" he asks, unfazed.

I nod to the cigarette. "Someone was here."

Catcher exhales sharply, and his gaze moves to the river. "Could have been a drifter."

"Maybe," I murmur, but anyone snooping around doesn't sit right with me. "I'll talk to Prez about beefing up security, just to be safe, more trail cameras, and some motion-activated floodlights."

We make our way back to the clubhouse, where our club girls,

Payton and Josie, are waiting inside. They look up the second we walk in.

"Find anything?" Payton asks.

"Nah," I say, not needing them to worry. "Get some sleep."

They hesitate, then head toward their rooms. I pull out my phone and dial Riggs. He picks up before the first ring finishes.

"What ya got for me, brother?"

I sigh, rubbing the back of my neck. "Someone was here, snoopin' around the shed near the river. No sign of them now."

There's a beat of silence, followed by a sigh. "Stay put for the rest of the night, just in case."

"Got it." I wait for the call to end, then glance across the room at Catcher, leaning against the bar with his arms crossed over his chest. His face is a mask of anguish, eyes shadowed and intense as if each thought is a silent scream. It looks like the weight of hell is crushing him, carving deep lines of worry into his brow and tightening his jaw in a fierce battle against the heaviness of his memories. But to be fair, he always looks that way. If I carried that amount of pain from a past like his, my exterior would reflect it, too. "I'm crashin' here for the rest of the night, but I need to grab my bike," I tell Catcher. "Parked it on the other side of the mill."

Catcher nods but doesn't speak.

I step back outside and roll my shoulders. The air is heavy as I move through the darkness, my senses on high alert. A feeling, the kind that settles deep in your gut before shit hits the fan, claws at me as I trek my way toward the mill.

I close in on my bike.

Then, an explosion rocks the ground, and a wave of energy slams into my chest, throwing me backward. I hit the ground hard, gravel biting into my palms. My ears ring, the force knocking the breath from my lungs. Heat rolls over me in a blistering wave as fire lights up the night like the gates of hell just blew open. The old mill is an inferno, flames clawing skyward along with thick black smoke. The scent of burning oil, scorched metal, and gasoline fills the air.

I push up, my vision swimming, blurred by the heat and smoke. I notice my bike lying on its side a couple of yards away. I get to my feet and make my way to it, needing to get it and myself away from the inferno. Not far from my bike, sitting on the ground is a red gasoline can that wasn't there when I left my ride earlier. I crouch, getting a better look, making sure not to get my prints on it.

But something else catches my attention.

Scrawled in thick black Sharpie on the bike's blue gas tank are the words '*Watch your back.*'

My blood runs cold as anger boils beneath the surface.

Sirens wail in the distance, indicating that authorities will be here soon, so I need to get the hell out of there before they arrive. The last thing the club needs is the cops sniffing around, thinking the Kings are linked to this.

Gritting my teeth, I maneuver my motorcycle off its side, gripping the handlebars tightly as I push it upright and back to the clubhouse—sweat clinging to me, thick with the stench of smoke.

Up ahead, under the streetlight's glow, I notice Catcher jogging toward me, his expression tight. "You good?"

"Yeah," I huff.

Catcher's gaze drops to my bike, his sharp eyes catching the message left on the gas tank. His head snaps up. "Who'd you piss off?"

My jaw flexes.

"Think the fire and the trespasser are connected?" Catcher walks beside me.

"Don't know."

Once inside the clubhouse, I yank my phone from my pocket and call Riggs again, and he answers immediately.

"What?"

"We might have a problem."

"Talk," his tone darkens.

"Someone blew up the mill. It's burnin' to the ground as we speak." I exhale. "And someone wrote 'Watch your back' across my bike's gas tank." There's a beat of silence before I add, "I think it might be linked to the fucker peddlin' pills we tossed out the bar the other night."

"What makes you think that?" Riggs questions.

"I had a second run-in with him and another pusher outside the boxing gym hours ago. He mentioned his boss wasn't too pleased with us interfering with his operations."

The silence stretches between us, thick with the weight of my information, filled only by the distant crackling of flames consuming the mill.

"This shit ain't sitting right with me," Riggs finally says, his voice cold and measured. "We need to find out who this pusher's boss is and find out whether that fire is just his men taking matters into their own hands or if they are, in fact, following orders." Riggs is quiet for a beat, then says, "I'll send out a message to the others. We're holding church at first light. Keep me updated should anything else happen."

I exhale slowly, nodding to myself as Riggs' words settle like a loaded gun in my gut. This isn't just about an asshole pushing drugs in the wrong bar or outside the youth center's gym. The drug problem has been making itself more prevalent for some time now, with dealers testing the waters by pushing boundaries. Even if the fire is just a coincidence, we're already in the thick of something bigger. "See you at church, Prez." I end the call.

Catcher stands beside me, arms crossed, eyes fixed on the distant glow of the mill burning. Without a word, we walk the property's perimeter again and check every inch of the clubhouse.

When we're satisfied that no one is lurking where they

shouldn't be, we climb up to the flat rooftop of the clubhouse. The vantage point gives us a clear view of the fire crews battling the blaze. The flames have died down some, but the old mill is a total loss. I stroll toward the fold-out chairs and drop into one, pulling a pack of smokes from my pocket. Flicking open my lighter, I take a slow drag before holding the pack out to Catcher. He takes one, lighting up and leaning back in his chair beside me.

We sit for a while, watching the fire crews work through the night.

Catcher exhales, his cigarette glowing in the dark. "If this is some unhappy drug lord, he's makin' a real fuckin' statement."

6

LONDON

I'm standing in front of a full-length mirror in my bedroom, getting ready to go out with the girls. After bailing on them the past few weeks because of work, the guilt has been eating at me, so I called Promise this morning and asked if she wanted to hang out tonight. After I hung up with her, my next two calls were to Sadie and Ruby, who were also on board for a girls' night.

I slip on a dark green leather mini-skirt and pair it with a cream-colored bodysuit and matching cream-colored leather boots. Once finished, I brush through my long black hair, letting it cascade over my shoulders. I keep my makeup minimal with a light layer of mascara and finish with a bold, dark red lip. I plan to forget my worries and focus on having a memorable night with my girls.

As I grab my purse and head out the door, I can't help but feel the buzz of excitement because as soon as Promise recommended we go to Twisted Throttle, my thoughts drifted to Everest. Everest is one of the brothers, meaning he's a member of the Kings of Retribution. He spends most of his nights at the bar owned by the club. Everest acts as a bouncer of sorts. He also lives in the apartment above the bar.

It's not that I'm not over the moon to finally see my friends, but I'd be lying if I said I wasn't looking forward to seeing that mountain of a man. Over the years, Everest and I have engaged in flirtatious banter, though mostly one-sided. Essentially, I like to give him a hard time. It's my nature. While everyone thinks I'm teasing, the truth is, I have a good old-fashioned crush on the guy. I'm just too chicken-shit to do anything about it. Generally because Everest, though friendly and shares the occasional jab, hasn't given any outward indication he's interested.

Upon arriving at the bar, I spot my friends sitting at a table at the back. I watch as all three faces light up when they see me walk in. *God, I love my girls.* As I move through the crowd, I notice Nova behind the bar and give him a friendly wave, which he acknowledges with a chin lift. I notice Everest standing at the end of the bar with his arms crossed over his broad chest the second I walk in, but I make it a point not to give him my full attention, though I can feel his gaze on me. It's hard not to when every time I'm within the same vicinity as the man, my skin tingles with awareness. It's all I can do not to trip over my feet as I approach my friends. My entire resolve fails before I reach the table, and like a moth to a flame, I turn my head and lock eyes with his, and because I can't help myself, I wink. I might be imagining things, but I swear I see the corner of his lips lift a little at my flirtatious gesture. Other than that, his face remains a mask of indifference. The interaction lasts only seconds before my attention is again on Promise, Ruby, and Sadie, who have all risen from their seats, ready to greet me with enthusiastic hugs.

"I'm so glad to see you!" Sadie boasts. "I feel like it's been ages."

"It hasn't been that long." I laugh.

"No, but when you hang out with five-year-olds all day, a couple of weeks feels like months." Ruby giggles. And even though my friends are joking, I can't help but feel guilty for neglecting them.

The sound of laughter and the clink of glasses fill the room as I settle into my seat beside Promise. "It's packed tonight," I note.

"Ladies." Nova personally brings us our beers and sets them on the table before wrapping an arm around Promise, pulling her from her chair, and laying the kind of kiss on her that most people would only give behind closed doors. But one thing I have learned about the men in the club is they don't play by the rules, and they sure as hell don't give a fuck what people think. I love this for my friend, though. I love seeing her happy and adore how Nova treats her. Watching them together, I can't help but feel a sense of melancholy. I've had a few relationships over the years, but nothing compared to what Promise and Nova share. To have a man who spends every day devoted to making his woman happy and ensuring she is cared for and protected, no matter the cost. As my thoughts wander, so do my eyes. Once again, I seek out the man who has held my attention for the past few years.

Jesus, London, you need to get laid so you can stop obsessing over that man.

As the evening wears on, the girls and I fall into our usual routine of getting drunk. Our laughter echoes through the bar and, a few times, draws the attention of male admirers who attempt to approach our table in hopes of flirting and getting lucky. However, according to Nova's orders, Everest has stood guard to ward off advances. It's not that Sadie, Ruby, and I don't enjoy the attention from time to time, but we have rules when it comes to girls' night, and one rule is absolutely no men. For the most part, we are left alone at Twisted Throttle because the regular patrons know Promise is off-limits, but because New Orleans is a tourist spot, it's not uncommon for the occasional dip-shit college bro to be put in his place.

"So." Sadie smiles at me and Promise. "How have things been at the office? Had any exciting cases lately?"

"Meh." I shrug. "Just your run-of-the-mill lying, cheating, asshole husbands."

Promise smirks. "Lon has been killing it lately in court. Since she made Mr. Davis lose it in front of the judge, which resulted in him spending a night in jail, we've taken on four new clients."

I take a sip of my beer and smirk. "Two of those clients were from the Reeves law firm."

"Damn, London, you're a savage." Ruby laughs.

"I do try," I say, flipping my hair over my shoulder.

"How's your mom been?" Sadie changes the subject, her tone softening.

I take a deep breath, feeling the familiar mix of sorrow and hope. "She's doing good. Mom has her good days and her bad. We make the most of the good. I'm grateful to the staff at Golden Hills who care for her. They are wonderful."

Sadie reaches across the table and squeezes my hand. "That's good to hear. It must be hard."

I nod, grateful for my friend's support. "Knowing she's safe and cared for helps a lot," I say.

"Well, if you ever need anything, you know we are here for you," Sadie tells me. "Even if it's just to talk."

I squeeze her hand in return. "I appreciate that, babe. Thanks."

Turning to Ruby, I ask, "How's work? How are the kids?"

Ruby beams at my question. "They're a handful as always."

One thing about Ruby is that when her time comes, she will be a fantastic mother. She truly has a heart of gold and loves children.

"Speaking of kids, has anyone talked to Vayda lately?" I ask. "How's the baby?"

Promise starts to gush. "Oh my God, he's an angel. I stopped by to see Tequila yesterday and to take her some pre-prepped meals for the week. Damien is such a good baby. She and Wick are on cloud nine."

"I'm so happy for them." I smile.

As the night progresses, we abandon our table and go to the small dance floor in front of the stage. A local band is playing tonight, and after getting a little liquid courage in me, I feel like dancing. The band plays a couple of fast-paced rock ballads that have me and the girls cutting up the floor. The four of us look absolutely ridiculous, but we don't care. We are not trying to win any dance competitions or impress any men. Behind the bar, Nova's shaking his head and grinning at Promise, who doesn't have a lick of rhythm but, by the huge smile on her face, knows it and doesn't give a damn. Then, my gaze roams across the floor toward the corner of the stage where Everest is posted. His focus is zeroed in on me, and he's not trying to hide it. I can't read the blank expression on his face, but there is no mistaking the heat in his eyes.

"Are you two ever going to stop pretending there's nothing between you?" Promise steps up beside me and bumps me with her hip.

I sigh. "That is one mountain I'd like to climb." I tear my eyes away from Everest and regard my best friend. "Over and over again."

Promise giggles. "I'm being serious, Lon."

I grin. "Me too."

She slaps my arm. "You know what I mean. I know you like him. And, by the way he's been watching your every move since you walked in tonight. I'd say he's into you, too."

I shrug. Everest has not indicated he's into me beyond our occasional flirtatious banter. Promise is right, I like Everest, but I don't like rejection. If I tried to go there with him, and he wasn't interested, that would make things crazy awkward moving forward. Promise will always be a part of the Kings' family, and because she's my best friend, I am too. There is no way to avoid Everest. Instead of telling Promise the whole truth, I give her part. "I have too much going on to think about a relationship." I look at Promise. "I need to be focused on my mom right now."

Promise's face softens. "I get it. I just want to see my best friend happy, is all."

I return her smile. "I'm happy enough."

"Oh, Lon." Promise pulls me in for a hug.

The band breaks out in a slow-tempo number a few seconds later. Ruby and Sadie rush to us, and Promise releases her hold on me, breaking up our moment. "I love this song." Sadie sighs as the four of us form a huddle and dance again.

Closing my eyes, I raise my hands above my head and move my hips to the beat. For a few moments, I can let all my troubles drift away. I forget how much I miss things before Mom got sick. I forget that instead of fulfilling her dreams, she is wasting away in that place. I forget how different her life could have been if she hadn't been forced to be a single mom. I forget how she gave up all her dreams to give me mine. But as soon as the song ends and the bar turns silent, all those thoughts come flooding back, and suddenly, I feel like I'm suffocating. The room spins, and my throat closes, causing me to choke on my next breath. I can feel sweat running down my temple as my vision blurs.

I look over at Promise, who is hugging Ruby, and the two of them are laughing at something Sadie is saying, but I can't hear their voices past the whooshing sound in my ears. Just as I feel like I will stumble and fall, a strong arm wraps around my waist, catching me. The smell of pine, leather, and cigarettes fills my senses.

"You're okay," Everest's deep voice rumbles against my ear, sending shivers down my spine. "Breathe, London," he commands. It's then that I realize I've been holding my breath. The next thing I know, Everest is ushering me outside. I look over my shoulder to see Promise, Ruby, and Sadie's worried expressions as Nova holds his arms out while keeping them in place. Promise's expression turns angry until Nova leans in close and says something against the shell of her ear.

Once outside, the cool night air blasts across my face, and I suck in some much-needed oxygen. Everest's six-foot-five-inch form crowds me, keeping the throng on the sidewalk at bay, for which I am grateful. To onlookers, I'm just another drunk girl to gawk at. I lean my back against the brick wall and brace my palms against the front of my thighs. "I don't know what the hell that was, but thank you," I say through ragged breaths.

"Panic attack," Everest murmurs.

As a cold bottle of water is shoved in front of my face. I don't question where Everest suddenly got it, I wipe my sweaty brow with the back of my hand. Instead, I take it from him and greedily down half its contents.

"Panic attack? I've never had one of those. How did you know?"

"Finish the water," he says without answering my question. Too freaked out to argue, I do as I'm told. After I finish the first bottle, Everest passes me another. I wave him off. "I think I'm good now."

"You'll be good once you drink this." He practically shoves the water in my hand, leaving me no choice. I give him my best annoyed look, but in true Everest fashion, he is unaffected. I go to bring the bottle to my lips when I notice my hand trembling. "Fuck," I hiss, leaning my head back against the wall.

"What's up with this chick?" A polo shirt wearing idiot asks as he passes by on the sidewalk, making his dickhead friends laugh. Normally, I have a witty retort for assholes like him, but I currently don't have the strength. I'm shocked when Everest swiftly reaches out, wraps his large hand around the guy's throat, and squeezes. I watch as the guy's face turns red. His buddies are equally stunned and do the smart thing by stepping back. I don't blame them.

Everest comes by his name honestly—a wall of muscle and stands at six feet five inches tall.

"Next time you walk by a lady on the street, you either show her some goddamn respect or keep pushin'," Everest growls, his face twisting with anger.

The guy claws at Everest's hand as his friends plead for Everest to let go.

"He didn't mean anything by it, man. Really. Can you let him go now?" one friend asks.

"Everything okay, brother?" Nova appears beside us, seemingly bored, with a cigarette hanging from his mouth.

Everest then releases the guy with a shove, and he falls to the dirty sidewalk. His friends crowd around him as he struggles to find his breath.

"We're cool. Just givin' this dip shit a little lesson in respect." Everest turns back toward me. "I'm takin' London home."

Nova regards me. "You doin' okay, sweetheart?"

I give him a weak smile. "Yeah." Then add, "Will you tell the girls I'm sorry and tell Promise I'll call her in the morning."

"Sure thing, darlin'." Nova and Everest share a look before Nova dips back inside the bar.

Grabbing me by my elbow to keep me steady, Everest leads me down the sidewalk to where my car is parked. "Wait." I try to stop. "I forgot my purse."

Everest raises his other hand and produces my small handbag. Nova must have handed it over, but with my attention on the exchange between Everest and polo shirt guy, I missed it. "You know, I'm feeling better. I can drive myself home."

Everest doesn't break stride. "Not happenin'."

We reach the passenger side of my car, where Everest opens the door. Once I'm seated, my eyes follow his trek to the driver's side, and I watch as he gracefully folds his massive form behind the wheel. There is no small talk on the drive to my apartment, yet surprisingly, the silence between us is comfortable. Soon, exhaustion sets in, and suddenly, I'm having difficulty keeping my eyes open.

I must have fallen asleep because the next thing I know, I feel like I'm floating on air, wrapped in a cocoon of muscle, heat, and that familiar smell of pine and whiskey. Cracking my eyes slightly, I mumble, "I can walk."

"I got you, baby." Everest's hot breath whispers against my ear.

I must be dreaming because I could have sworn I heard him call me baby. *Yep, definitely dreaming.* And because this is a dream I don't want to wake up from, I bury my face against the column of Everest's neck and breathe in his scent. "Mmm, you smell good," I murmur. In my dream, a deep rumble vibrates against my cheek. "I love it when you growl, too. It's so hot."

"Fuck," dream Everest grits.

I yawn. "I think I like that too, mountain man."

A few moments later, I'm lowered into my bed. Briefly, my eyes flutter open to find Everest standing at my bedroom door, staring at me. "Well, that's not creepy at all." I give him a lazy grin.

Everest shakes his head.

"Good night, Everest."

"Night, baby."

7

EVEREST

The city fades behind me in a blur of stop lights and taillights as I throttle my Harley onto the open road. New Orleans' usual mix of music, car horns, and pedestrians soften to a low hum in my rearview. In its place comes the steady roar of my engine, the rush of the wind, and the swampy perfume of the bayou.

Each mile I put between me and the city loosens the tension in my body as the bike's vibrations seep into my bones. Cypress trees paint the landscape, their branches draped with Spanish moss, or what some call Old Man's Beard, swaying in the humid breeze. Behind me, the sun is sinking lower, painting the sky in swirls of orange and purple as I drive down the two-lane blacktop that snakes through the swamp. Out here, it's just me and my bike. The solitude and freedom of the road, working their magic on my soul.

Its tranquility also allows thoughts I've been trying to shake to take root, all swirling around one person.

London.

I scowl and twist the throttle, trying to outrun her image. I lean into the road's curves, focusing on the horizon as the hot, sticky air rushes past me, carrying smells of brackish water and wild jasmine. It fills my lungs and pushes out the remaining unrest.

For now.

When I cross the old bridge and turn down the gravel road to Pop's place, I've almost found a semblance of peace again.

Pulling up to Pop's house, I cut the engine. I'm greeted by the lazy symphony of the bayou at dusk—crickets, tree frogs, and the distant call of a heron. Beyond the old man's home, parts of the water's surface glow with the last light of the day. The smell of charcoal smoke and grilled meat hangs in the air, making my stomach rumble. I roll my shoulders and breathe in the familiar scent of a Kings' gathering. And it looks like I'm the last to arrive.

I swing my leg off my ride and set the kickstand. Voices and laughter drift from the backyard and porch. I spot Riggs standing by a smoking grill, his arm slung around Luna's shoulder as she balances their daughter on her hip. He's flipping burgers, possibly steaks. Whatever it is, it smells damn good. A few feet away, Wick is holding his and Tequila's newborn. In the distance, I see Nova and Kiwi tossing logs and various-sized tree branches into a pile for a bonfire. At the far end of the dock that stretches over dark water, I notice Catcher standing alone, hands in his pockets, looking out at the bayou like he's searching for answers in the murky darkness.

I stroll across the yard, making my way to the house, and stop by a cooler near the front porch steps. Lifting the lid, I grab an ice-cold beer and pop it open. I take a seat on the steps and dig out a cigarette. A few feet away, Pop is rocking gently in his chair, the wood creaking with each sway. Deep lines are carved into his tanned, weathered face.

"Evenin', son," he greets me.

"Hey, Pop," I reply, flicking my lighter and taking the first satisfying drag of my smoke. The nicotine hits my lungs, and I exhale slowly, feeling the last remnants of tension from the ride slip away. I raise my beer and take a long pull. The cold washes down my throat, cutting the summer heat a notch.

From my spot, I can observe damn near everything. The whole family, my brothers and their women, all scattered around enjoying the evening. Through all the chatter and laughter, the low tunes of some easy, laid-back classic rock play.

The screen door squeaks behind me, and out steps Piper, Kiwi's woman, and London. London is carrying two wine glasses in one hand and a bottle of red in the other, laughing, the sound ringing in my chest. The late sunlight catches her from behind, holding her in a warm glow. For a beat, I watch her. She's wearing cut-off denim shorts that show her toned legs and a black tank top with thin straps. Her wavy, dark hair tumbles over her shoulders.

I realize I've gone still, with my beer halfway to my mouth, just staring at her. London has a way of snaring my attention without even trying. Every damn time I'm around her.

I drag my gaze away before anyone notices. Still, after London and Piper make their way toward the other women, London looks back over her shoulder, like she feels me, her eyes flicking to mine. I feel the jolt. It's like a live wire crackling briefly, with an unspoken charge passing between us. My fucking pulse kicks up, and I give her a slight nod, keeping my face neutral.

London's eyes linger half a second longer before she breaks from the spell and turns away.

Behind me, Pop lets out a low chuckle.

I clear my throat and take another swig of beer, the liquid doing nothing to cool the heat coursing through me. Pop's rocking chair creaks steadily, and I feel his eyes burning a hole through my head.

"She's a firecracker, that one," Pop says, his voice low enough not to carry beyond us. He doesn't have to say who he's referencing. I already know. "She's easy on the eyes, too," he adds.

I huff and rub my jaw. Pop is not wrong. That fire London has is one of the many things drawing me to her, and there's no denying she is easy on the eyes. That being said, there's something more to Pop's words, something weighty.

I don't trust myself to comment, so I grunt in agreement and take another drag of my cigarette.

I turn, leaning against the post, where I can see Pop, whose gaze is locked on me like he's got more to say. I exhale, the smoke curling upward, waiting for his words.

"You know." His voice is low and steady. "A man can spend his whole life riding free and think he's got everything he needs until he looks back one day and realizes something is missing." He pauses to let his words sink in. "That gal has the kind of spirit that'll mend a rough soul, but only if the fool holdin' that soul is brave enough to take a chance."

My shoulders tense up. Pop may as well have reached over and thumped me on the back of the head. My gaze strays across the yard to London, and my chest tightens with the all-too-familiar tug. "Don't know what you're talkin' 'bout."

Pop chuckles. "That lie is thicker than my mornin' bowl of grits."

I chuckle and shake my head at the old man's no-nonsense straightforwardness. "Is that so?"

Pop then clears his throat. "Mhm. That gal got a weight in your chest. It's as plain as the nose on my face."

"Ain't got nothin' to offer her." My tone is flat.

"Sure, you do. And you better figure out if you're gonna fight it or fall into it, 'cause the kind of pull I see between you and London doesn't come around often. And if you fuck around and wait too long, some other bastard might feel it too," he says in a tone that is both advice and a gentle warning.

I clench my jaw. His words hit a target I've been dodging for months. "I hear ya," I murmur, keeping my voice low. I tip my beer back, but the bottle is nearly empty, and the taste has gone warm. I stub out my cigarette, letting the silence eat up between us, grateful Pop doesn't push further. I stay here on the steps, turning the empty bottle in my hands, my attention shifting across the yard again, and this time London's gaze is locked on me. I feel the same pull in my gut and fight the same urge to get up and approach her. Instead, I stay rooted where I sit.

A couple of hours later, after the sun is fully set and the fireflies light up the shadows, we circle the bonfire in mismatched chairs, some old folding ones, and a few stumps Pop cut years ago. Fender has a fresh beer in his hand, and Jo is curled beside him. Tequila is relaxing in a chair beside Wick, who's half asleep with his arm slung around her shoulder. Like always, Nova and Promise are tucked together, and Piper's got her legs draped across Kiwi's lap. Me? I'm leaning back in my chair, one boot propped on a pile of unburned logs, watching the flames flick and lick at the sky while Fender recounts one of our road stories.

"This fucker had eaten three gas station burritos." He chokes back a laugh.

Kiwi throws both hands up. "Come on, mate."

"He was sweatin' like a sinner in church before we even hit the highway," Nova adds, laughing.

Fender continues, trying to keep a straight face. "We're ridin' down this pitch-black backroad. Middle of nowhere, and suddenly, Kiwi peels off the road, jumps off his bike like it's on fire, and heads straight for the trees, yellin' code brown."

Tequila chokes on her drink, which startles Wick.

Nova's laughing so hard he damn near spills his beer.

"He disappears into the tree line, no flashlight. No TP. Twenty minutes passed before he came walking back, looking like he'd been to war, holdin' his boots in his hands and no fuckin' socks on."

The entire group erupts. Catcher is doubled over, Nova wipes tears from his eyes, and Riggs laughs while signing what's being said to Luna, who shakes her head and signs '*disgusting.*'

"I was blowin' napalm and prayin' for mercy. Nothin' but soft cotton was touchin' my pucker button after that, so I offered up my socks like a goddamn sacrifice."

London's gaze catches mine mid-laugh and lingers momentarily before shifting away. Her face glows in the firelight, her lips slightly parted, her eyes fixed on the flames, and she gets lost, like she is a thousand miles away.

What's that all about?

London stands, brushing her legs. "And on that note, I think I'm gonna call it a night," she says lightly. "Not feeling great."

Promise frowns. "You sure?"

"Yeah." London nods. "I have a long day ahead of me tomorrow, so..." her voice trails off.

I'm not buying it.

For weeks now, she's been dipping out early, avoiding people, slipping away like she's got something to hide.

Maybe she does.

That thought sits like a fucking rock in my stomach.

I don't want to care.

I shouldn't.

But I do because, like it or not, she's got her hooks in me.

While the rest of the crew shoot the shit, I sit silent. I wait, giving London time to get some distance before checking out myself.

When I think enough time has passed, I stand. "I'm out."

Kiwi eyes me. "First London, now you? Somethin' you not tellin' us, mate?"

"No." I do my damnedest to keep my tone neutral, not wanting to stir up more speculation and curiosity than I already am by leaving.

"Stay safe," Riggs says, leaving it at that.

I nod. "Always."

I turn my back and stroll across the yard, heading for my bike, the whole time feeling the weight of everyone's stares.

The sound of my engine tearing through the night makes my leaving anything but subtle, but I don't give a fuck. I only have one thing on my mind—*London.*

I have no trouble catching up to her car, but I keep my distance, far enough back that she won't notice me shadowing her. As we near the exit back to the city, she blows right by it.

Where the hell is she going?

A fucked-up feeling coils in my gut as I consider the possibility that she's meeting some bastard. Again, it shouldn't bother me, but it does, and it gets me thinking about Pop's words from earlier.

I grit my teeth and try like hell to push my frustration away because if she slips through my fingers, I have no one to blame but myself.

I tail her for another thirty minutes before she slows and flicks on her turn signal. So I ease off the throttle, watching her pull into a parking lot with a neon sign glowing against the darkness, casting a dull red glow over the lot.

Pink Paradise.

A fucking titty bar.

What the hell is London doing here?

I ease my bike off the road, pulling over just off the lot, parking in the shadows of an old gas station across the street.

I watch her. She doesn't hesitate to get out of her car. She steps out like she's been here a hundred times before, slinging her bag onto her shoulder and walking straight for the entrance. I even notice her smiling at a large motherfucker handling the door and the way he looks at her, tells me they've met before.

Heat starts in my gut and rises into my chest.

And I realize I'm fucking jealous.

I clench my jaw so tight that my teeth ache.

I wait a while before cutting my engine, swinging my leg over my bike, and jogging across the road. My gaze drifts over the property. Outside, the place appears clean enough, nothing high-end, but not a total dive. It looks like the kind of place where the floor won't stick to your boots. I stroll up to the entrance, reining myself in as I approach the guy standing there. He's a big motherfucker. But I'm bigger. He eyes me with a stone-cold neutral expression, saying nothing. I take out my wallet, pull out forty bucks, confident that it more than covers the door fee. He takes the cash and jerks his head.

The lights are low inside, and bass-heavy music pumps through the speakers.

I sit in the back, close to the door but out of sight. I scan the room, searching for London, but she's nowhere to be seen.

"Hey, handsome," a voice purrs beside me.

I turn my head slightly, catching sight of a pretty little waitress with a tray balanced on her hip, giving me a sweet smile.

"Get you a drink?"

"I'm good," I say, my voice clipped. It's not rude, just not interested.

She takes the hint, giving me a wink before sauntering off.

I lean back, pulling out a smoke and lighting up as the lights dim even further. A hush falls over the crowd. You can feel the thick anticipation as the stage glows red.

A sultry beat pulses through the speakers.

"Witch Woman."

A figure struts onto the stage, bathed in the crimson light, long red hair cascading down her back. She's wearing something tiny, red lace and barely there straps, the kind of outfit meant to make a man forget his goddamn name.

She moves like sin, hips rolling slow, hands sliding over her curves as she grips the pole, arching her back. Her body is a fucking work of art as she puts on a show that has every man in the room riveted.

Including me.

I can't look away.

There's something familiar in the way she moves, tilts her head, and how her body flows with the music.

Then she turns.

Those eyes pin me to my seat.

London.

My whole body goes tight.

She's been sneaking off to this?

I'm shocked at first, but it's quickly replaced with something hotter, more possessive, and primal than I care to admit.

I watch her move and own the stage with raw sensuality, and fuck if it doesn't do something to me.

The fact that this is her secret doesn't sit right with me. I don't know her reasons, but I'm damn sure going to find out.

London finishes her set and disappears backstage. I don't stick around. Instead, slipping out the way I came, stepping out into the warm night air, my pulse still thrumming from what I just watched.

I don't leave.

I wait, hidden in the shadows across the road, watching until London finally emerges a couple of hours later, with her long dark hair pulled back, and gets in her car. I wait for her to pull out of the parking lot, letting her ease down the road before tailing her back to her apartment in the city. I keep my distance, watching as she slips inside the safety of her home.

I should ride off and head back to my place, but I don't. Instead, I sit on my bike, the engine running, staring at the building like I've got unfinished business. And I do.

Because the woman I've been keeping at arm's length, fighting every damn instinct not to make her mine, is moonlighting as

Raven, drenched in red lights, grinding on a stripper pole for other men, and hiding from everyone. That alone is enough for me to keep my eyes on her.

My jaw tightens as I light another smoke and tell myself the secrecy is eating at me. I tell myself I need to keep London safe, but the truth is much deeper and much harder to admit.

I want to see Raven again.

I want to be the only one watching her move like that.

And that makes me a selfish bastard.

But I don't give a fuck.

Whether she knows it yet or not, London is *mine*.

I flick the ash off my cigarette.

Until she's ready to tell me why she's doing this, I'll bide my time and keep her little secret.

8

LONDON

"Your eleven o'clock had to be canceled, and she wants to know if she can come in at two." Zara's soft voice draws my attention away from my laptop. I offer her a kind smile as she timidly knocks on my office door. A few months ago, Promise brought up the idea of hiring Zara as an assistant at the firm. A couple of years ago, Zara and her son, Julian, fled Mexico with the help of Vayda, her team, and the Kings. She was the wife of the now-deceased cartel boss. Over the past couple of years, the Kings have put her under their protection. She and her son have thrived in their new life in New Orleans. Before working here, she worked as a cashier at Rusty's Buy & Bag. Unfortunately, Rusty's closed down four months ago, leaving Zara unemployed. The dilemma worked out well for her and us because Zara has been a godsend. She is dependable, efficient, and speaks Spanish, which has broadened our client base.

"Yeah, tell her two o'clock is fine. Thanks, Zara."

Since my schedule has changed, I break for lunch early. I skipped breakfast this morning and know if I don't eat soon, my head will kill me later. Pushing away from the desk, I power my computer off and grab my purse. Across the hall, I see Promise is still not back from court, so I decide to ask Zara if she'd like to go to Maggie's with me. Walking down the hall, I pass the break room and find Zara heating food in the microwave. "What do you say you ditch the leftovers and come with me to Maggie's? My treat."

Zara looks down at her bowl of what looks like rice and chicken while biting her bottom lip. Over the past several months, Promise and I have worked diligently to get Zara to open up and trust us. Considering her history, I don't blame her for being wary of people. Finally, she gives me a small smile and tosses her container back into the refrigerator. "Okay."

"So, how's your little guy doing? Promise mentioned last week, he started a new daycare. Is he adjusting well?" I ask Zara on our drive into town.

Zara beams at the mention of her son, Julian. "Yes, he's settling in. Everyone there has been so nice and understanding. I'm grateful to Mr. and Mrs. LeBlanc for getting him in at Fun Friends & Frontiers."

Apparently, Julian's last daycare kicked him out due to behavioral issues. Zara had been beside herself. She and her son had both had their fair share of challenges since leaving Mexico, but she had been handling them head-on and with grace. Julian's daycare's unwillingness to work with Zara had been a tipping point, though. But in true Kings fashion, the club used some connections and helped. They got Julian into a new daycare, and he now sees a child therapist three times a week.

As I pull into an empty parking spot in front of Creole Café, I recognize the white Honda Accord parked two cars over. I see Ruby sitting at a table on the sidewalk in front of the restaurant through the windshield. A smile spread across her face, and she waves when I exit my car. "Fancy seeing you here."

"I had a client reschedule, so Zara and I decided to take an early lunch."

Ruby brightens up. "Perfect. You two can eat with me."

I look at Zara. "You cool with that? You remember my good friend, Ruby, don't you?"

Zara tucks a strand of hair behind her ear. "Of course. It's nice to see you again, Ruby."

"It's nice to see you, too, Zara. How's Julian?" Zara replies as the two of us take a seat across from Ruby.

"He's good. Mrs. Bethany started teaching him the alphabet this week. She said Julian is one of her brightest kids."

I can hear the pride in Zara's voice when talking about her son.

"That's fantastic!" Ruby rushes. "It would be a dream to have your sweet boy in my class when he starts kindergarten."

The conversation is halted when Mrs. Maggie bursts through the door of her restaurant carrying a tray loaded with sweet tea and her famous rye bread and honey butter. "London. Ruby, Zara! What a blessed day it is to see you three here."

"Hey, Maggie. How's it going?" I ask.

"Shoo, child. Other than these achin' knees. I can't complain. Now, what will it be today, ladies? Danny's red beans and rice will knock your socks off."

"Perfect. Red beans and rice it is. I'm going to need some bread pudding, too," I tell her.

"Same for me," Ruby follows.

Zara nods. "I'll have that too. Will you give me some extra bread pudding to go? I want to take some home to my little boy."

"Sure thing, honey. I'll be back in a jiff with your order."

Just as Mrs. Maggie scurries back inside, the familiar rumble of a motorcycle draws our attention, and the three of us watch Catcher park his bike beside my car. Catcher tied himself to the Kings not long ago and is now the club's latest prospect. He seems like a good guy, but I can't seem to get much of a read on him. I feel there's a story behind his sad eyes, though. Catcher is all hard lines and a mask of indifference, but there's no mistaking the pain he carries around on his shoulders.

"Hiya, Catcher," I greet him as he strides past our table. Catcher stops briefly and slides his shades from his face to the top of his head. "Lon," he replies with a nod. His gaze then sweeps the table before halting on Ruby, who has suddenly turned three shades of red. With a tip of his chin, Catcher disappears inside the café.

I turn to Ruby with a lifted brow. "What was that?"

Ruby's blush spreads to her ears. "What was what?"

My eyes narrow as I watch her pick at the bread on her plate. Beside me, Zara giggles.

"Ruby, do you have the hots for Catcher?" I tease.

Ruby sputters, "No!"

"Oh my God. You totally do!"

"What are you, five?" Ruby tosses a piece of bread at my face, making me laugh.

My teasing comes to a halt when Catcher exits the café. He slides his shades back down over his eyes and tosses a nod our way as he walks past our table.

"Good seeing you, Catcher." I wave. "Right, Ruby?"

A foot connects with my shin underneath the table, making me grimace. "Ouch. That hurt, heifer."

"I'm going to kill you," Ruby whispers.

"Guys, look." Zara nudges me with her elbow.

Ruby and I peer down the sidewalk at Catcher perched on his bike, head turned toward us.

"Great," Ruby mutters. "He probably thinks we're idiots."

With a shake of his head, Catcher fires up his motorcycle and takes off down the street.

"You're the worst, Lon," Ruby grumbles once Catcher is out of sight.

"Meh." I shrug. "You love me anyway."

Ruby pops a piece of bread in her mouth and continues to pout. "Unfortunately."

After lunch, Zara and I arrive back at the office. The rest of the day is blurry with one client meeting after another. It's nearly six o'clock by the time I make it home. I had plans to visit Mom, but when I checked in on her an hour ago, her nurse said she was sleeping and would probably be down for the rest of the night. I told them I'd stop by first thing in the morning before heading into the office to have breakfast with her.

I'm walking through the door to my apartment when my phone chimes with a text. The screen lights up, revealing its Journey. I inwardly groan because Journey texts only when she wants me to switch shifts with her. I'm too beat to work for the club tonight and contemplate ignoring her, but decide against it. If Journey needs me to take her shift, it would be for a good reason, and I can't leave her hanging like that. But when I tap on her text it's not what I thought it would be.

Journey: *Amara was a no-show tonight. I'm worried about her.*

A chill runs down my spine as I read the words.

Me: *Maybe she's sick. Did you try calling?*

Journey's reply is instant.

Journey: *Yes. I called and left a voice message, and I texted several times, too. She hasn't responded.*

Me: *Did you talk to Tony?*

Journey: *Yes. You know him though. He said he'd take care of it. I'm worried, Lon. I'll go by her place tonight and see if she's there.*

"Damn." I blow out a breath. I could try to talk Journey out of going and letting Tony handle things, but I feel she won't listen. We've all rallied behind Amara to help her get away from her asshole boyfriend, and so far, she has shown no signs of going back to him since he gave her a black eye a couple of weeks ago. Her not showing up to work has me concerned.

Me: *Where are you?*"

Journey: *I'm at home. I've got one of the other girls to take my shift so I can look for Amara.*

I close my eyes and tip my head back toward the ceiling. "This is a bad idea, London."

Blowing out a breath, I text Journey back.

Me: *Send me your address. I'm coming with you.*

Ten minutes later, I head out the door after changing out of my work clothes and putting on a pair of jeans and a T-shirt. I follow the GPS directions to an older but well-maintained neighborhood about fifteen minutes outside New Orleans. When I pull into a driveway, I spot Journey climbing down her porch steps toward my car.

"You know Tony is going to kill us if he finds out what we're doing," I remark as she slides into the passenger seat.

"What Tony doesn't know won't hurt him," Journey replies.

The address Journey has for Amara leads us to a not-so-great-looking neighborhood. Amara once mentioned she inherited her grandparents' house when they passed. I imagine years ago, this was a neighborhood that thrived, but now it looks run down.

"I think this is it." Journey points to the small yellow house to our right. I park across the street and cut the engine. Journey and I don't exit the car right away. I survey the surrounding houses and note that Amara's is the only one that looks kept up. The grass is cut, and a small flower bed is out front. The house is not much to look at, but Amara has taken pride in her yard. The sun has set, but there is no porch light on at Amara's house, and the streetlight I'm parked under doesn't work.

"What are you thinking?" Journey asks.

"I don't know. I say we knock on the door and see if she's home."

Just as we are about to exit the car, the front door to the house swings open, and two men wearing suits walk out.

"Fuck," I hiss. "Get down." Journey and I crouch down.

"Shit, Lon. You think they saw us?"

When I chance a peek out the windshield. A black SUV appears out of nowhere and rolls to a stop at the end of the driveway. Then I watch the two men who just came out of Amara's house climb into the SUV.

"I don't think they saw us. They're gone."

Journey sits up. "What now?"

"We get the fuck out of here," I say. "I don't know what's going on with Amara, but I don't have a good feeling."

Suddenly, a shadowy figure appears at my driver's side window, causing us to scream. The figure leans down, showing their face.

"Jesus fucking Christ," I say, clutching my chest when I see Tony's angry face through my window.

"You two get your asses to the club now," he orders, then walks away before we can argue.

Journey slumps in her seat. "Shit."

The ride to Pink Paradise remains silent because we know we are in for an ass-chewing from Tony. That is precisely what Journey and I get when we walk into his office. We sit across from his desk and listen as he lectures us.

"Did I or did I not tell you two to let me handle this situation with Amara?"

I go to open my mouth when he points a finger at me. "Zip it. You're lucky those men didn't spot you. Damn lucky because I clocked your asses the second you turned onto the street."

"Really?" Journey scrunches her nose. "We didn't see you."

"That's because I know how *not* to get caught." Tony grinds his jaw. Then he turns his attention toward me and continues, "I brought you in on this because I trusted your judgment. Was I wrong about you?"

I sit up straighter in my chair and narrow my eyes. "No. But Amara is our friend. If she's in trouble, I will do whatever I can to help. And if I'm to be her legal counsel, I need to be involved."

Tony's demeanor diminishes slightly at my declaration. "I understand, but you and I both know what you did tonight was not smart. If something happened to you, that would be on me."

I blow out a breath and rub my temple. "I can admit that what Journey and I did was reckless. It's just... what if something terrible has happened to Amara?"

"I'm on it, London." Tony holds my stare. "I have a guy following a lead as we speak. We will find her." There is no mistake in Tony's tone. "Now, I want you two to go home and stay there," Tony finishes.

9

EVEREST

After making a quick trip to my apartment, I return to today's event, the grand opening of the youth center's boxing gym.

The hum of laughter and music rolls down the block. It feels like the whole damn neighborhood showed up. The place is packed with vendors and families. A bounce house sits in the back corner, already leaning like it's taken a few too many roundhouse kicks from sugared-up kids.

It's a hell of a sight.

The club and our community showed up in full force today. It's good to have people willing to protect, build, and give back. This gym will become a good foundation, a shot at something better for this community and kids who often don't get second chances or even first ones.

The new sign on the building now reads Hope Youth Center & Boxing Gym in bold letters. Seeing it sends a swell of pride through my chest. This is what all those long nights were for, and it feels damn good to see it finally come to life.

The women are in full force today, too. Luna and Tequila are set up inside the gym with their little ones, selling raffle tickets to win family fun packs to the Audubon Nature Museum and Zoo, as well as a family movie night fun pack. Across the parking lot, near the bounce house, Piper is helping a local animal shelter with adoptable dogs, while nearby, Jo and her daughter, Sawyer, are busy face painting with Payton and Josie helping. My gaze drifts to where Promise, Sadie, and Ruby are stationed, serving up all the grilled food being cooked by Riggs, Nova, and their old man.

My gaze drifts, searching for one particular person. Then I catch a glimpse of her and fight back a smile that she is here. My eyes stay locked on London as she smiles warmly at an elderly man waiting for a food tray.

I tear my eyes off London and glance down just in time to see a wild-eyed kid sprinting past, shrieking joyfully.

"Watch where ya goin', Jacob, and keep the water wars in the field," Charlie bellows across the lot at the kid, towing a wagon full of ready-to-use water balloons.

"Sorry," a kid shouts as he bolts, his hands wrapped around a couple of water balloons.

I chuckle as Charlie trudges past me while Kiwi approaches.

"You're fightin' a losin' battle, mate," Kiwi says, then takes a bite of the mustard-smothered hot dog in his hand.

"What are you goin' on about?"

Kiwi points across the parking lot. "London."

I grunt, saying nothing but not denying it either. It's not like I can argue because he's right. And the battle has amplified since discovering London's little secret.

Nova strides over, holding out a couple of cold beers. "The place looks damn good, brother."

I nod and look toward Charlie, who referees a group of kids, grabbing as many water balloons as they can take from the wagon. "Charlie deserves most of the credit." I grab the bottle of beer from Nova and take a sip. "Charlie gives the center much more time and energy than I do. The community and kids are the soul of this place, but Charlie is the heart of it."

Riggs claps his hand on my shoulder, pulling me from my thoughts. "Hell of a crowd."

Wick joins us. "Nothing brings people together like free food." His tone is light, but beneath the surface lies a palpable tension.

We fall into a tense silence, the chatter, joyful laughter, and pulsating music swirling around us, failing to penetrate the weight of unease in the air—my gaze darts across the crowd, searching for anything or anyone out of the ordinary. We're here for the kids, but the looming shadow of the mill fire lingers in our minds, alongside the message warning me to watch my back. It's been quiet lately, but silence can be a prelude to danger in our world. So, we remain on high alert.

I catch sight of a familiar face standing near the corner of the building, Jace. He's shifting from foot to foot, his eyes fixated on the ground. I haven't seen him since the night I busted him with those two drug pushers. My gut tightens with a mix of relief knowing he's okay, and fresh anger that he even entertained talking with those motherfuckers in the first place. "I got something to take care of," I mutter and break away from my brothers, weaving between a cluster of sticky-faced kids by the baked goods table, heading in Jace's direction. When I'm near the corner of the building, he finally looks up.

His eyes widen slightly, and he straightens. "Everest." His voice is low and unsure as his eyes dart nervously.

"Jace." My tone is steady, giving nothing away yet.

Jace clears his throat. "I thought I'd come to look at the gym now that it's finished." He tries to smile, but it falters under my stare.

I cross my arms over my chest. "Wasn't sure I'd see you again."

Jace drops his gaze and rubs his hand over his neck.

I study him, keeping my face impassive. I've known Jace for a few years now. I've seen what he's been through with a deadbeat dad, a mom working two jobs, and the pull of local gangs constantly gnawing at his door. "Those guys you were talkin' to the other night, they still around?"

"I've seen them in the neighborhood a couple of times." He locks eyes with me. "But I swear I haven't fucked with 'em."

"You know what they do, right?"

"Yeah," he mutters.

"You want that life?"

"No," he quickly replies, but I'm not buying it.

"You got a lot stacked against you, kid. Your old man is doin' time for the same shit those two pieces of shit you were talkin' with are involved in. I know that's a shadow hanging over you, but you don't have to live under it."

"I'm not selling or buying." His tone hints at anger while defending himself.

"Doesn't matter. When you're seen with pushers, people start makin' assumptions."

His jaw ticks. "I'm not my old man."

"Then don't make the same choices he did."

Jace sighs. "They came to me. I didn't want trouble, so I listened to what they had to say. You know, show a little respect, they tend to leave you alone."

I shake my head. "Respect doesn't mean standing next to a pile of shit, hoping you don't smell like it. Get what I'm saying?"

Jace shoves his hands in his pockets. "I get it." He nods.

"Good." I clasp my hand on his shoulder, giving him a firm squeeze, letting a beat of silence hang between us to stretch the moment. "You eat?"

"Not yet," he replies.

With a nod, I draw back a little, still holding his gaze. "Go grab some grub and put some meat on them bones."

Watching him walk away, my thoughts drift back to our

conversation. The drug pushers are still hanging around the neighborhood. I can't let them sink their claws into the kid. But I know the streets—nothing's ever that simple. I know that for Jace, each day feels like he's teetering on a razor's edge with his choices. Every day is a balancing act for him, risking everything with each decision. I exhale slowly, tasting bitterness, hoping that when he faces tough choices, he finds the strength to choose a better path, avoiding prison or, worse, an early death.

I watch Jace making his way across the parking lot, then turn and head back to the guys, but stop mid-stride and drink in the sight of London, who's just a few feet away at the clothing donation table. She's standing in front of a large fan, sunglasses perched on her head, black hair pulled up in a messy bun, with a few rebellious strands curling down the side of her neck. She's wearing cut-off shorts and a Hope Youth Center T-shirt. Nothing over the top, but it shows off her toned legs and hugs her curves in ways that make it damn near impossible to look away, even though I've seen more skin than this.

She turns, catching me eyeing her.

There's a beat of silence between us, not uncomfortable, just thick and unspoken. It's almost like she's reading my thoughts. The sound of the crowd fades, and for a half second, I feel the same pull I always feel when she's around, like gravity is getting stronger.

London speaks up, and I prepare for the usual sass. Instead, she surprises me with, "It's an incredible turnout."

"Not gonna bust my balls?" I respond blandly.

London smirks. "You want me to?"

I'd rather be balls deep in you. The thought sears my brain, and by the look on London's face, I'm questioning if the words fell out of my mouth.

London huffs, crossing her arms under her breasts. "I'm trying to be nice. I know what this place means to you."

"Seen the inside yet?" I ask, leaning into the pleasantries she's dishing out.

"You offering to give me a tour?" She studies me.

"If you're willin'."

"I'll lead the way." London saunters toward the entrance, her hips swaying slightly.

The second we step into the gym, the shift in sound is noticeably quieter. I spot Luna and Tequila at the back of the room and feel their eyes tracking our movement as we walk around the ring. London walks beside me, taking it all in.

London scans the room. "Why boxing?"

I look at her. "It requires discipline. You have to follow the rules and learn respect. It encourages kids to think about themselves and others. This place can provide a refuge for kids when the temptations in the streets start whispering in their ears. I know it won't save everyone. But it might save one. That's what matters."

Her gaze lingers on me for a beat longer. There's something in her expression I can't quite read. Whatever it is, it's softening the edge she usually wears like armor.

I gesture to the ring. "You ever box?"

London smiles. "Only in court."

I chuckle. "I believe it."

We start walking the floor, passing walls lined with framed photographs of the kids we've helped and come to know over the years, along with headshots of famous boxers for inspiration.

"This is impressive," she says, rolling her hand along the bottom rope and momentarily pausing. "I enjoy giving you shit, Everest, but I'm sincere when I say your dedication to the kids in this community is commendable."

Outside, the noise swells as Charlie's voice cracks through the megaphone. He is about to announce the raffle winners.

With that, the tour is over.

London and I drift toward the door, sunlight slapping us in the face as we step out into the hot, sticky southern, no-mercy kind of heat. A ripple of laughter explodes nearby. Then, out of nowhere, a swarm of kids charges past like a damn stampede.

I react on instinct. My hand clamps around London's waist, hauling her against me just as a kid barrels too close. Her body crashes into mine, her soft curves press against my chest, and fuck if it doesn't short-circuit my brain.

London gasps, her hands braced against me and her eyes snapping to mine with surprise. Her pupils dilate, and her lips part like she's about to speak but can't find the words.

I keep my hand on her waist, feeling the heat of her skin burning through the thin fabric of her shirt.

I should let her go.

But I don't.

Neither does she.

We're locked in. Everything around us fades. It's just the two of us in this charged second. Right now, all I can think about is how good she would taste if I leaned in and kissed her.

"Lon." A voice cuts through the moment like a blade.

I tear my eyes from hers and see Promise waving from across the parking lot, where the rest of the women are gathered under the shade of a couple of tents, all laughing and sipping on something cold.

I look down at London. She blinks, the spell broken, and steps back, slipping from my grasp and putting distance between us and what almost happened. Without speaking, she turns, walks away and doesn't looking back.

My jaw is tight, with every muscle in my body wound like a goddamn spring as I watch her go.

Kiwi walks up with a tray full of baked goods and a gigantic grin. "She's got you by the balls, mate."

I grunt and turn my attention back to London, tracking her as she joins the women.

"Here, have a cookie, brother. Sometimes, it helps to eat your feelings." He chuckles and nudges the tray at me. "Don't worry, big guy, we've all been there."

Jesus fucking Christ.

I don't say anything and snatch a motherfucking cookie off the tray. Remaining silent, my gaze still on London, I wonder what I'd have done if Promise hadn't interrupted, and contemplate what the hell I'm supposed to do about the woman taking up too much space in my head.

Later that night, we all hang out at Twisted Throttle, unwinding from a long-ass day. My brothers and their women have all claimed their usual spaces. The bar is alive with chaos, music, and muffled conversation. It's loud, rowdy, and familiar.

It's a good night.

We earned it.

With a beer in one hand, I stake out my usual spot near the entrance, leaning against the wall as laughter swells and the music intensifies. I scan the room through the haze of smoke and the scent of spilled beer. My senses are heightened, and I watch for anything amiss because I can't shake this undercurrent of tension. It feels like a storm brewing just beneath the surface.

Needing a breather, I step outside, light a cigarette, and exhale the smoke into the thick New Orleans night. As always, Bourbon Street is alive. I watch a group of musicians pack up and drag their battered instruments down the sidewalk.

Upon hearing the clicking of heels, I glance to my left, spotting a woman pulling away from some tatted frat boy and heading in my direction. She has long legs, painted lips, and is wearing a dress that belongs in a backroom.

"You sure are a hard man to miss." Her eyes run the length of my body like she's already undressing me.

I take another drag, staring straight ahead. "Ain't lookin' for company."

She smirks, stepping closer, invading my space. "Maybe not, but you're getting it anyway." Her hand grazes my arm when a voice cuts through the street noise like a blade.

"Oh, sweetie," London calls from behind, her voice dripping with sarcasm. "He's not into women who smell like cheap perfume and desperation."

The woman looks around me at London, her arms crossed, locked and loaded with attitude. She's wearing confidence like a second skin and the kind of smile that promises trouble.

"Who the hell are you?" the woman spits.

London tilts her head. "Oh, I'm just the woman who can spot a thirsty trainwreck from a mile away. You must be exhausted chasing attention in those heels all night."

The woman snorts. "Jealousy looks ugly on you, sweetheart."

London doesn't blink. "Not as ugly as those crusty feet and ratchet dress."

I damn near choke on my breath. The way London slices with that mouth of hers. *Jesus.* I almost feel bad for the woman. I don't say a word. I keep my expression neutral and let London do what she does best by setting a fire and walking away without blinking.

The guy the woman left behind finally notices she is not at his side. "Hey." He angrily strides over and jabs his finger into my chest. "You trying to take my girl, bro?"

I flick my cigarette away and sigh. I do *not* have time for this shit. I stare at the dumbass.

He steps closer. "You think you're better than me?"

"Absolutely," I mutter.

He swings.

Or tries to.

I sidestep, grab his shirt collar, and slam him into the wall hard enough to make his head crack against the brick. "You want to walk away," I say quietly. "Or you want to leave here without teeth?"

He struggles against my hold, trying to shove back, but he's sloppy. The bastard's pride is writing checks his ass can't cash. "Fuck you." He spits, then looks right past me at London. She's standing there, arms crossed, with a half-smile on her lips. It's not for him, but it's enough to set the motherfucker off. He sneers. "What the fuck are you grinning at, whore. Why don't you get over here and suck my dick, bitch."

My vision flashes red.

One punch.

His nose shatters beneath my knuckles before his head jerks back, then down before his body crumples, out before he hits the concrete.

I stare down at him, blood already trickling from his nose. My breathing is slow and tight, my fists still clenched at my sides, and my pulse hammering in my ears. I didn't hit the fucker for me. I did it because I'll be damned if a man spits filth, disrespecting London. No one talks to her like that. Not on my watch.

I shift my gaze to his woman, frozen nearby. "Get him the fuck out of here."

She hurries to wake him, muttering curses while giving the asshole a couple of slaps to his face to rouse him. When he finally comes to, they walk away.

London lets out a slow breath. "Well, that was subtle."

I glance at her. "If you hadn't been out here marking your territory, it wouldn't have happened."

"Excuse me?"

"You heard me."

"I was trying to help."

"Didn't need it."

London steps closer. "You didn't look like you minded. I'm willing to bet you enjoyed it." She calls me out.

There's heat in the air.

It's not from the weather or the fight.

It's from us.

London steps back, her eyes dancing with something more than the sass she's throwing my way. "Let the others know I'm out for the night."

"Runnin'?" I challenge why she's leaving.

"From what?"

"You tell me, babe," I press, holding her in place with my stare.

She doesn't answer—simply glares at me before turning and walking away.

And just like every other time I watch her, my mind is racing with everything I keep bottled up.

London isn't mine yet.

But mark my words, one of these nights, she will be.

10

LONDON

Sitting in court, watching Judge Hoffman's face turn red, fills me with giddiness. I have to keep that shit under wraps, though. I keep my expression neutral. I can't say the same for the opposing counsel sitting to my left. I'll admit, I don't feel bad for Marsha Drexler. I don't feel bad for any woman who would go against the girl code and stand beside a piece of shit, man.

Marsha's client, Adam Kiefer, has been subjecting his ex-wife to a long and drawn-out custody battle involving their two-year-old son. The former Mrs. Kiefer, now Ms. Baxter, had been diagnosed with breast cancer while pregnant with their son. Mr. Kiefer wanted her to end the pregnancy, seeing as it wasn't planned, and he didn't want children. Ms. Baxter, however, chose to keep her baby and forgo any treatment for her cancer until the baby was born. Her prognosis hadn't been good. Not to mention, Mr. Kiefer filed for divorce when she was seven months pregnant.

I represented Ms. Baxter in her divorce, where she received a hefty settlement along with the judge's order for her estranged husband to continue paying all her medical bills, including her cancer treatment, after their son had been born. Ms. Baxter has remained steadfast through it all. She gave birth to a beautiful, healthy boy alone. Underwent treatment for her breast cancer alone. Endured a grueling divorce alone. For the past eight months, she has been fighting for her son, a son her husband never wanted, but has decided to fight for just to hurt my client even further. But today, Mr. Kiefer slipped and showed his true colors by not bothering to show up to court, a true testament that he didn't care about his son.

"Your Honor." Marsha stands. "I'd like to call—"

Judge Hoffman holds up his hand, effectively cutting Marsha off. Now, Marsha's face turns red from embarrassment. "Save it, counselor. You and your client have wasted enough of my time, which was demonstrated in my courtroom today. I'm granting full custody of two-year-old Lucas Baxter to his mother, Mary Baxter, along with the requested child support. Mr. Kiefer will also be required to pay all back child support." The judge finishes by slamming the gavel.

"Thank you, Your Honor." I stand.

Judge Hoffman offers a warm smile. "Best of luck to you and your son, Ms. Baxter."

Beside me, Ms. Baxter holds her hands clasped together in front of her chest with silent tears running down her cheeks. I can't help but feel a sense of pride mixed with admiration as I look at this incredibly strong woman in front of me. I'm proud to be standing on the side of what's right. Unfortunately, we live in a world where the bad guys win more often than not. But on days like today, when justice prevails and victory is sweet, it makes taking on all the asshole Adam Kiefer's of the world worth it. Watching scum attorneys like Marsha lose is an added bonus.

After court, I stop by Maggie's to pick up the to-go order I phoned in fifteen minutes prior, then head to see my mom. When I arrive at Golden Hills, I'm greeted by her nurse. "Hey, London. I see you brought lunch today."

"Hey, Mary. Court ended early, so I thought I'd bring Mom her favorite from Maggie's." I hold up the bag. "How is she today?"

Mary's face softens. "She's a little lost today, but other than that, she's good. I can take you to her if you like. She's enjoying the sun out on the lawn."

"That would be great. Thanks, Mary." I follow Mary outside and spot Mom sitting in an Adirondack chair facing the lake.

"She likes to watch the ducks," Mary tells me. "Faye, you have a visitor."

As we approach, Mom's head turns toward us. My chest tightens when she peers up at me without a hint of recognition.

"Hello," she greets me in a way you'd greet a stranger. "Do I know you?"

I swallow past the lump in my throat and smile. "No. But I saw you sitting out here by the lake and was hoping you'd like to share some lunch with me."

"That sounds lovely." Mom's eyes light up.

Mary smiles warmly before taking her leave.

Sitting in the chair beside Mom, I dig the Styrofoam container out of the bag.

"Whatever that is, it sure smells good," Mom says.

I open the container and show her what's inside, and that's when her eyes light up like a little girl. "Mac and cheese is my favorite. How did you know?"

The ache in my chest returns. "Lucky guess," I croak, setting the plate in her lap and settling her with a plastic fork and napkin. Macaroni and cheese was a staple in the Monroe household growing up. Mom said mac and cheese was a cure-all, and it truly was. Nothing in the world would cure a bad day at school, a scraped knee, or a broken heart like mac and cheese.

One day, when I was seven, I came home from school in a mood after Bobby Markle pushed me down on the playground at recess and stole the sticker Mrs. Nelson had given me for finishing all my homework. Mom sat me down and gave me a bowl of mac and cheese, then explained that Bobby was just jealous because I was an A student. And she gave me permission to kick him in the balls if he ever put his hands on me again.

Then there was the time when I was fourteen. My boyfriend broke up with me the day before the winter dance and asked Beth Arnold to go with him instead. Again, Mom sat me down with a bowl of mac and cheese and taught me that if a boy treated me the way Connor had, he wasn't good enough for me. It was better to find out early if a boy was worthy of my time rather than finding out later.

Mom was right.

She was always right.

And the mac and cheese ritual didn't stop as I grew older.

When I was in college, if I was having a crap day, I could come home to my mom, and she'd have a plate prepared for me by the time I walked in the door, along with her words of wisdom.

God, I miss those days. I want to be back in my childhood home with my mom after a bad day and have her tell me everything will be all right. My life is a mess, and I struggle to stay above water every damn day.

Mom is sick, my friend is missing, and I'm looking my best friend in the eyes every day and lying to her because I'm ashamed of the things I have to do in order to take care of the woman who means the most to me in this entire world. I feel like a fraud, a failure, and a shit friend. I just want to eat mac and cheese and have my mom take all my troubles away. But that's not going to happen. And the reality of that is hitting me like a ton of bricks.

When I look over at Mom, she's greedily eating on her food in silence while watching the ducks swim around in the lake. I can't help but stare at the woman sitting next to me and think how unfair life is. How can the woman sitting here look like my mom but at the same time not look like her? You would think the days when she's angry and doesn't understand who she is or where she is are the hardest. They're not. It's days like today where her eyes are void of the light she used to exude. Days like today are when she's the shell of the person she once was. She looks lost. But that's what the disease does. It takes and takes until you have nothing left to give.

I'm taking a bite of my food when Mom's hand pauses halfway to her mouth. She looks at the fork and then down at her plate. She's silent for a beat before she turns and looks at me. And just like that, I see a familiar light shining in her eyes.

"London."

"Hi, Momma," I whisper.

Mom blinks. "I was lost again, wasn't I?"

"That's okay, Momma. You found your way back." I sit my plate on the grass beside the chair and then drop to my knees in front of my mother. My eyes close when her shaky hand cups my cheek. "I'll always find my way back to you, Doodlebug," she says, using my nickname.

"I know you will, Mom," I reply when the first tear falls. "I know you will."

The last thing I want to do after visiting Mom is be around people. I have a shift at the club tonight, and all I want is to go home, take a long bubble bath, and maybe take a nap. But when Promise calls and asks if I want to stop by Twisted Throttle for a beer, guilt creeps in, and there is no way I can refuse.

By the time I stroll into the bar, it's already five o'clock. I smile and wave at Nova behind the bar, cleaning glasses as he prepares for the six o'clock rush of people who stop by after a long day at work. I scan the room and spy Promise sitting at a high-top table in the back, along with Luna and Riggs. Over the past couple of years, I have committed myself to learning ASL on Luna's behalf, so when I approach the table, I sign, "Sorry, I'm late. I was visiting Mom, and the traffic was a bitch." I lean in, kiss Promise on the cheek, and do the same with Luna before greeting her man. "Hiya, Riggs."

Riggs does that macho man chin-jerk thing. "London."

Before I'm fully in my seat, Nova sets a beer down in front of me. "Here ya go, darlin'."

I let out a sigh. "I need this. Thanks, Nova."

"Bad day?" Luna signs.

I take a pull of my beer. "Work is good."

"How's your mom?" Promise asks. I shrug and start picking at the label on the bottle. I don't want to tell them it fucking sucks to watch someone you love slowly drifting away because then I'll start crying, so I remain silent. Silence sometimes speaks louder than words, though.

"Fuckin' sucks about your ma, sweetheart." Riggs breaks the silence.

I give him a wobbly smile. "Thanks."

Seconds later, the room's atmosphere shifts the same way it always does when *he* is around. I don't have to turn to know who's just walked in, but I do anyway. And when I peer over my shoulder, my gaze connects with Everest. His face is hard, and a mask of indifference is perfectly in place. His eyes, however, turn molten, burning into me. So much so that I feel it between my legs and my breath hitches. Beside me, Promise makes a noise, and my head snaps toward her. My best friend is wearing a knowing smirk. I roll my eyes, ignoring her, and go back to my beer.

Luna lifts her hands and goes to sign, but is effectively cut off when Riggs' lip twitches as he shakes his head. "Leave it be, Mon Tresor."

My friends are convinced there is something between Everest and me. I don't see why they think that. Or maybe I do, and I'm in denial. At this juncture, it doesn't matter. I have too much on my plate to be worried about a man. Everyone I care about is currently living their happily ever after. Everyone but me. And because those people love me, they want me to find my own Prince Charming.

After the failed attempt to hound me about Everest passes, the conversation takes a lighter turn when Piper makes an appearance. "Piper, where have you been? Tell Kiwi he needs to let you up for air more often."

"Jesus fuckin' Christ," Nova bitches. "I don't need to hear that kind of shit."

I smirk as Nova makes a face and takes his leave. Riggs matches his brother's energy and follows suit, causing Piper to turn red and groan. "You know you're scaring my dad for life, don't you. I bet his ears are bleeding right about now."

"I know." A giggle escapes from my lips. "I like making Nova squirm, though."

Piper hugs me and then falls on the stool beside me. "I've been MIA the past couple of weeks, but school is keeping me busy," she says loud enough for her dad and uncle to hear.

"When is graduation again?" I ask.

"Three months." Piper beams. "I'm so ready."

"Your dad and I are so proud of you." Promise reaches across the table, squeezing Piper's hand. There is no denying the bond that Piper and Promise share.

Over the next hour and forty-five minutes, the girls and I catch up on what's going on.

Looking down at my watch, I note the time. "Well, ladies, I hate to cut our time short, but I have to go."

"So soon?" Promise grumbles.

"Yeah. I have to stop by the grocery store on my way home, and I have a mountain of laundry I need to do. If I don't, I'll have to show up to court tomorrow in sweats and a T-shirt. I'm pretty sure that sort of thing is frowned upon."

Promise goes to grab her purse. "Want some help? I don't mind."

"No!" I rush the word out, causing Promise to look at me with wide eyes.

Recovering, I wave my hand. "I mean, I'm fine. No biggie."

"Okay." Promise eyes me skeptically. "As long as you're sure."

I lean in and give her a hug. "I'm sure." Then I turn toward Luna and Piper and sign. "I'll catch you ladies later."

Piper and Luna bid their goodbyes before I take my leave.

As I'm walking out of the bar, I sense familiar eyes on me. My skin tingles with awareness, only this time, I don't look.

Pink Paradise is packed tonight, and the patrons are growing increasingly rowdy. Or should I say, the group of guys here celebrating a bachelor party? Bachelor parties are the worst! Meaning, for some reason, they have in their tiny pea brains that said party entitles them to behave like creeps. On more than one occasion, Royce has had to remind them to keep their grimy paws off the girls. Tony has a strict no-touching rule, even regarding private dances. He also has a three-strike rule, and this group has used up two of their strikes. I block out their insinuating gestures as I finish my last dance. Launching myself at the pole, keeping my legs wide as I skillfully complete a full twirl before flipping my body upside down. I wrap my legs around the pole, then thrust my chest outward as I run my hands along my breasts while my fake red hair dangles down toward the stage.

I catch a flash of movement from the corner of my eye right before one of the imbeciles from the bachelor party rushes the stage. His buddies whoop and holler. Panic sets in, and I lose my balance. My grip on the pole gives, and I crash to the stage. "Fuck!" I cry out when a sharp pain shoots up my tailbone.

The next thing I know, all hell breaks loose.

Just before the lights go out, I see a large figure tackle my would-be groper. The girls working the floor scream and scatter down the hall toward the dressing room, while I'm hauled up off the stage by Royce, who picks me up with ease.

"Oh my God! What the hell just happened?" I twist in Royce's arms to get a look at all the commotion, but all I see are chairs being thrown and people scrambling to get out of Dodge.

Once in the dressing room, Royce sets me on my feet. "Nobody leaves this room," he booms before slamming the door shut. The girls and I stare at each other.

Journey rushes to my side. "Girl. Are you all right? That was one hell of a fall you took."

"My ass feels like it's on fire, but other than that, I'm okay." I walk over to my locker, pull out my jeans, and pull them over my G-string. I don't bother with a bra as I slip my T-shirt over my head. There's something too vulnerable about standing around half-naked, so I don't waste any time getting dressed. Plus, after what just happened, there is no way Tony won't shut down for the rest of the evening. The other girls follow suit and begin cleaning up and getting dressed.

Twenty minutes later, Tony barges through the door, his face red with fury. He scans the room until his eyes land on me. "You okay, sweetheart?"

"I'm good, Tony."

"I'm fuckin' sorry that shit went down. I should have kicked their asses out sooner. This shit is on me."

"It's all good, Tony. Promise."

"Fuck no, it's not. Nobody hurts one of my girls. He's gonna pay."

Before I can ask Tony what he means by that statement, he

changes the subject. "Club is closed. And don't worry about tips. I've got you covered. You girls get on home. Give Royce fifteen, and he'll escort you to your cars."

"Tony." I stop him before he leaves. "Any news on Amara?"

Tony's face turns grim, his lips thin, and he shakes his head. "Not yet, but I'm workin' on it."

I close my eyes and let out a sigh. *Maybe I should try looking for her again.*

"I know what you're thinkin', and I'm telling you right now, London, to leave this shit to me. The only thing you need to do is take your ass home. Like I said, I'll catch you up to speed when my guy finds somethin'."

I narrow my eyes at Tony, but my expression doesn't faze him.

"Tell me you got me so I can go clean shit up."

"I got you, Tony."

Tony then turns on his heel and disappears down the hall without another word.

I sling my bag over my shoulder with no other reason to hang around.

"Wait, Lon. Are you not going to wait for Royce?" Journey calls out.

"Nah. I'm beat and have an early day tomorrow. Later," I say with a wave as I make my way down the hall toward the back exit. Though I'd prefer the night not to end in drama, I'm thankful for the few extra hours of sleep I'll get tonight. I've been running on fumes for months.

A warm breeze hits my face when I swing open the door. As I make my way to my car, an eerie feeling washes over me, and suddenly, I wish I'd waited on Royce like Tony instructed. He's adamant that we girls don't leave the club alone. Halfway to my car, I look over my shoulder, scanning the near-empty lot, and breathe a sigh of relief when I don't see anything. My relief is short-lived when I twist back around and come face to face with a man I don't know but have seen once before. He's one of the men Journey and I saw come out of Amara's house last week during our failed stakeout.

"Nighty, night, bitch," he sneers right before he presses something to my neck.

Then it's lights out.

I crack my eyes open some time later, feeling disoriented. Blinking several times, I try to force my muscles to move. As my vision finally clears, my eyes lock on an unfamiliar tattooed hand and a steering wheel. My gaze flicks up, and then my memory comes flooding back. Terror sets in when the asshole turns his head and looks at me with his chilling eyes. Bile rises in my throat as I try to force myself to do something, anything, but for some odd and terrifying reason, my muscles are unwilling to cooperate.

In that instant, I know what real fear is.

It's then that two things happen at once.

First, the car stops at a red light, and about ten seconds later, the driver's side window is busted out. Broken pieces of glass go flying, causing a scream to escape my mouth.

"What the fuck," my kidnapper spits while making a move for his gun.

The next thing I know, a beacon of hope in the form of a gaudy blue and green windbreaker is there. Tony's fist comes barreling down through the shattered window before slamming into the side of my kidnapper's temple, knocking him unconscious. I stare in shock at the man slumped over in the driver's seat. Moments later, the passenger door is ripped open.

"Let's go, sweetheart. Time to make haste before the cops show." Tony wrestles me from the car, practically taking all my weight, considering my muscles feel like mush.

"I don't know what's wrong with me," I say.

"That son of bitch stun-gunned you. You'll be all right in a few minutes."

We reach Tony's car, and he shoves me inside without a word. He sprints around the hood, then drops into the driver's seat, slamming the door shut. That's when I spot the baseball bat—no doubt the one he used to smash the kidnapper's window. He tosses it into the back seat like it's nothing.

"You're a pain in my ass, you know that?" he mutters, stomping on the gas. He runs a red light, the roar of sirens rising in the distance. We cut through backstreets and tight corners, avoiding the main roads. Every few seconds, Tony glances between the rearview mirror and the road, jaw tight, eyes sharp.

"What the hell just happened?" I ask in a panic.

"What happened is you didn't wait for Royce to walk you to your car like I said, and you got yourself kidnapped. Royce and Journey saw the whole damn thing. Saw that son of a bitch stun gun you and toss you in his car."

"You say that like I wanted this to happen." I narrow my eyes.

"No, I say that like you're a pain in my ass because you're a *pain in my ass*. And you *don't listen*."

"Whatever," I grumble. When I notice Tony is taking us back to the club, I add, "Shouldn't we go to the police?"

Tony shakes his head. "Not my call."

"Then whose call is it? Because you'd think when a person is kidnapped and stun-gunned, the only call to be made is to the cops."

Tony pulls up to Pink Paradise and twists in his seat. He gives me a look I'm not sure I like. "You're gonna be pissed but know I did this because I care about you. And right now, some serious shit is goin' down. I also know once you're done being pissed, you'll realize it was the right move."

Confused, I shake my head. And before I can open my mouth, a familiar rumbling sound echoes in the distance. The sound draws closer, so close that the windows on Tony's car begin to rattle.

Panicked, I ask, "Please tell me you didn't, Tony."

"London, the shit goin' down is not good. You could have been killed tonight."

Turning back to Tony, I shove the car door open and jump out, jogging across the strip club's parking lot toward my vehicle, but stop when I realize I don't have my keys or purse. *Dammit!*

Before I can think of an escape plan, six Harleys roll into the parking lot of Pink Paradise. A gamut of emotions washes over me, shame being one of them. These men are like family. Nova is married to my best friend. Everest is... well, I don't know. I just know I don't want them seeing me here, and I don't want them in *my business.* I have struggled for months to ensure this part of my life didn't bleed over.

I feel Tony at my back but refuse to acknowledge him. Instead, I watch Riggs, along with Everest, dismount their bikes. Riggs keeps his focus aimed at the man behind me. However, Everest locks eyes with me.

"You, Tony?" Riggs asks. Over his shoulder, I notice Wick, Nova, Fender, and Kiwi standing beside their bikes, each man on alert and ready for anything.

"That's me," Tony replies.

"Well, Tony. You mind tellin' me what the fuck is goin' on and why our girl is standin' here with you outside a titty bar?"

"I called you because I know what London is to the Kings," Tony boldly admits.

"Again, you wanna tell me how it is you know that, seeing as I don't know you?" Riggs counters.

"It's my job to know everything about my girls. Knowin' means I can do my part in keepin' them safe. Keepin' them safe means when London gets stun-gunned and kidnapped on my watch, I call you."

Everest's back goes ramrod straight. "The fuck you just say?" he spits, his tone lethal. I also notice the other guys' demeanor shift.

Tony switches his attention to Everest. "That's right. Shit went down about fifteen minutes after you dipped."

Stunned by his last statement, I whip around and snap, "What are you talking about, Tony?"

Tony nods toward Everest. "Your man. He's been here every night."

My mouth falls open. *Everest knows.* And just like that, I see red. Stomping over to Everest, I point my finger at his chest. "Have you been following me?"

Everest grinds his jaw but doesn't say anything.

Tony, however, does. "A man has to keep an eye on his woman. That's the way of things. I don't like boyfriends hangin' at the club while their girls work, but I was makin' an exception."

My head rears back. "I am *not* his woman," I shout at Tony.

Tony doesn't look convinced. "She yours?" he asks Everest.

"Yes," Everest answers at the same time I say, "No."

"Are you high?" I gape at Everest.

Again, Everest ignores me. Instead, he demands more answers from Tony. "Where the fuck was Royce when London was taken?"

Tony's expression turns to one of guilt. "He was handlin' somethin' for me. I told the girls to wait before leaving, but I should have known London wouldn't listen. She's good at *not* listenin'. I take full responsibility."

"You know I am right here, and I am a grown-ass woman who's responsible her own actions," I interrupt.

"Now is not the fuckin' time to be throwin' your personal brand of sass around, London," Everest growls.

My fists ball up at my sides. "You're not the one being talked about like you're not standing right here, Everest. And you are not the one who was stun-gunned and kidnapped tonight either. So, excuse me for being just a tiny bit pissed off."

"That's enough!" Riggs barks. "Tony, I want you to brief me and my men on what you know so my club knows what the fuck we're dealin' with." Riggs looks at Everest. "Brother, go sort your woman out."

"Prez." Everest jerks his chin.

Without another word, Tony leads Riggs, Wick, Kiwi, Nova, and Fender inside the club, leaving me standing here with Everest. "I don't care what Riggs said, I don't need to be sorted out. As soon as I find my keys, I'm going home."

"The only place you're goin' is with me," Everest informs.

"Go to hell," I sneer, fully aware I'm being a bitch. I can't help myself. I'm embarrassed, scared, and confused. Being a bitch is all I have to hold on to at the moment.

"London, if you don't get your ass on the back of my bike, I'll put you there myself. The choice is yours."

Everest and I stare at each other in a silent battle. The truth is, I know he's not bluffing.

"Fine," I concede, snatching the helmet from his grip before climbing on behind him. "I hate you," I mumble.

Everest calls me out on my lie. "No, you don't."

He fires up his bike, drowning out my racing thoughts and leaving no more room for argument before he peels out of the parking lot.

Rather than taking me home to my apartment, Everest brings us to Twisted Throttle, where he parks in the alleyway behind the bar. Wordlessly, Everest grabs hold of my arm and leads me up the stairs to his apartment.

"I can walk on my own." I try to wrench my arm away. "And I told you to take me home."

"You're not goin' home. You're stayin' with me so I can keep an eye on you."

Everest walks through the door of his apartment and flips the light on.

I take in the apartment—it's an open-floor concept with a small living room and kitchen. To my right is an open door that leads to the bedroom, and off the living room are double doors that lead out to a balcony. Surprisingly, the place is clean and tidy. There are no dirty dishes in the sink or clothes strewn all over the place. Beside the sofa is an end table and a stack of worn paperbacks.

"Time to start talkin'," Everest says, drawing me out of my perusal of his apartment.

"About what?" I ask.

"Now is not the time to play dumb, London. I want to know what the fuck you've gotten yourself into that would cause some motherfucker to stun gun then kidnap you."

"Fine. But why don't we start with why you have been following me and why you have been coming to Pink Paradise?"

"We're not talkin' about me." Everest starts to lose patience.

"Oh, I'm talking about you." I throw attitude back.

"Goddammit, London," Everest growls. "Why are you always a pain in my ass?"

"Why have you been following me? What makes you think anything I do is your business? Hmm?"

Everest takes two long strides across the living room, stopping within inches of my face. His intoxicating scent surrounds me. The man is two seconds away from losing his shit, and for some reason, it's doing funny things to my stomach. Not to mention, other parts of my body are suddenly waking up. His gaze flicks down to my chest as if he knows exactly what I'm thinking. I mentally curse the fact that I'm not wearing a bra because my nipples are rock-hard. Just like that, the fury in Everest's eyes turns heated.

My breath hitches, drawing his attention away from my breasts to my mouth. "Everest," I breathe.

"Fuck it," he says then his mouth is on mine. The instant his lips collide with me, I lose all resolve. All of a sudden, Everest breaks the kiss, and he's dragging me to the bedroom. We clear the doorway, and the next thing I know, my back is against the wall, and his rock-hard body is flush against mine. Before I can blink, he rips my shirt off over my head, exposing my bare breasts.

I grab a fistful of his hair, forcing him to look at me. "To be clear, I still hate you."

Everest smirks. "Let's see how much you hate me when I'm making you come all over my cock."

"I like it better when you don't talk." I push his cut down over his shoulders. "I can think of better things you can do with your mouth."

"I better get to work then," he says, then drops to his knees.

In the next second, my pants are shoved down over my hips, and Everest's mouth is on my pussy. "Oh, God," I gasp.

He runs his tongue along through my slit before his mouth latches onto my clit, causing my toes to curl. His hands glide up over my hips, along my belly, until they reach their intended destination. Large palms cover my breasts, his thumbs brushing over the tops of my nipples, making me toss my head back on a moan. Everest continues to eat at me like a man starved. My lips part in a cry when he takes his mouth away. "Your pussy tastes like fuckin' heaven, but right now, I need to fuck you."

"Good," I pant. "Because I need to feel you inside me." At my confession, I fumble with the button of his jeans while he rids himself of his shirt. Everest is all broad shoulders, tanned skin, and six-pack abs. He has an array of colorful ink covering both arms, but the skin on his chest remains bare. With hooded eyes, Everest watches me take in every inch of his body. Once I have my fill, I lean in and run my tongue along his corded neck. Using the wall as an anchor, Everest grips me under my thighs, lifting me off the floor. In one fluid motion, his hips shift, and the head of his cock nudges my entrance. Eyes locked on mine, Everest slams into me. There's nothing gentle about it, and no taking it easy. What it is, is utter bliss. The moment he's in, Everest buries his face in the crook of my neck and lets out a strangled curse.

Threading my fingers through his hair, I dig my nails into his scalp, press my lips against his ear, and whisper, "Fuck me."

Chest heaving, Everest tears his face away from my neck. He presses his forehead against mine and begins to move. He gives me exactly what I asked for. My back hits the wall with each powerful thrust.

"I knew it," he says, his tone low and husky.

"Knew what?" I ask.

"That tasting your pussy would be my undoing. And now that I've had a taste, my decision is cemented."

I bite my bottom lip. "What decision?"

Everest thrusts, knocking a cry from my lungs. "That you're *mine.*"

A shudder passes through my body when he says those three words. Everest must feel it, too, because all of a sudden, his movements intensify. "You like the thought of being mine, don't you, baby?"

The voice in my head screams *yes*, but when I open my lips, a lie escapes. "No."

Everest smiles in a way I have never seen before, and it is beautiful. "Liar."

Damn. How does he do that?

"You're *mine*, London, and one day soon, you're going to admit it." Everest slips his hand between our bodies and presses his thumb against my clit, making me see stars. "Now be a good girl and come for me. I want to feel your pussy drench my cock."

My words are a lie, but my body knows the truth because as soon as the command is spoken, the most intense orgasm wracks my entire body.

11

EVEREST

The morning light slices through the curtain, sharp and unforgiving. The air in the apartment still hums with the tension from the night before, while the scent of vanilla and sin lingers on my skin. And even though my dick is ready for round two, he'll have to wait because I want answers.

London is curled up at the edge of my bed, her back to me, her hair spilling over her bare shoulder like ink on white sheets. I've been watching her for some time, even though she's no longer sleeping.

I see the tension her body is holding.

I know her.

This woman's holding back.

Holding in what happened between us last night, and then some.

So am I.

Because while she might think last night started here in my bed, it didn't.

It started well before.

Even before I walked into that goddamn strip club and saw her dancing.

The truth is, I've been watching her for days, sitting in the shadows, making sure no one got too close to what's *mine*. To make sure she was safe. And telling myself I have no damn right to feel the way I do.

Then, a drunk asshole with more booze than brains stumbled to his feet and reached for her. He touched her like he had the right to do so. I was already moving before I realized it, shoving past tables and bodies, ready to break the stupid fuck in two. The bouncer got to London first, yanking her off the stage.

She didn't see the rest.

She didn't see me dragging the son of a bitch out the back door.

She didn't see the way my fist connected with his face repeatedly until my knuckles were slick with his blood.

I don't even remember if I said anything to him.

The rage took over, and I only wanted to send a message.

I was mid-swing when my phone buzzed in my pocket and I almost didn't answer.

I wish I hadn't.

It was Riggs. He needed me at Kings Tactical. The alarm tripped, and he was en route. So were the others. I cursed, left the bastard I was dealing with bleeding behind the dumpster, and reluctantly headed back to town, thinking I'd be back before the club closed its doors, and I could follow London home.

When I arrived at the store, it looked like a crime scene. A fire truck was parked out front, lights flashing, and the crew was still milling about. The fire marshal was also present. Smoke was curling from the open door. The sprinklers inside had done their job and extinguished the flames. Chief Richards was there speaking with Riggs. He wanted to know if the fire was just some random electrical issue or if the club had gone and pissed off the wrong person.

I fucking stood there, jaw tight and frustrated, trying to calm the storm in my chest the entire time because I couldn't shake an uneasy feeling.

Then Riggs got a call.

London was in trouble.

We didn't wait for details.

We just followed Riggs.

But I already knew where he was leading us.

I should have been there. If I were, London wouldn't have been stunned by a goddamn taser and tossed in a car like she was nothing. She wouldn't have been taken.

The only thing that saved her was the strip club's owner, Tony, who pulled some hero shit and got to her before the fucker had gone too far. London was saved. The fucker who attempted to take her was long gone by the time we got there.

And all of it is on *me*.

Every damn bit of it.

I'm the one who should have been there.

But I wasn't.

I sit up, the mattress dipping under my weight. My head is a mess of relief, anger, and questions. Last night was a climactic disaster of fire and fury. A collision of raw need and frustration. But it didn't solve shit. It only added fuel to the fire, trying to consume us.

It's time we stop fucking around.

No more hiding.

It's time for truths.

I stand, not bothering with clothes, and stride into the kitchen to make coffee. After it's done brewing, I grab a couple of mugs from the cabinet, fill them, add some sugar and cream to

London's, and stalk back to the bedroom. I sit her cup on the nightstand and stand there, watching her. She doesn't budge.

"Time to talk, babe." My voice is low and rough.

London shifts, eyes still closed, refusing to look at me, her jaw tight. "There's nothing to talk about."

I chuckle, but it's humorless. "Bullshit." I take a sip of coffee. "You gonna tell me why you've been sneaking around? Why you're dancin' half-naked for other men?"

Her eyes snap open, fire flashing in them. "I don't owe you answers." She pauses, then asks, "Why does Tony think I belong to you?"

I give her some truth, hoping she'll do the same. "Because I've been at the club, keeping my eyes on you since the night I found out you were stripping," I admit, and watch the storm swirling in her eyes.

"How long?"

"Since the cookout at Pop's."

"Let me make it perfectly clear. I don't belong to you, Kallum," London fumes.

I sit my mug on the nightstand and hover over her. London's eyes go straight to my dick, but I ignore it. "You. Are. *Mine*. Babe. From the moment I claimed you in front of my brothers to the second you let me inside you last night, you are *mine*."

London sits up, the sheet falling to her waist, exposing her breasts. She doesn't cover herself. I don't expect her to. Her eyes bore into mine. "Don't twist this." She waves her hand between us. "Last night was nothing. It meant nothing."

"Was it nothing?" I stare her down.

Her lips press into a thin line, but her eyes, defiant as ever, flash with something deeper. Something she's terrified to admit.

"It meant something, babe. You know it." I confront her with the truth. "Now, why are you stripping?" My voice is softer, but no less commanding, as I return to my previous question.

London snatches her coffee from the nightstand, wrapping both hands around the mug like a shield. Her eyes drop, and for a second, I think she won't answer, that she'll completely shut down and push me away.

But then she whispers, "I had to."

Silence settles between us.

It's thick and heavy.

"Why?" I press her.

London doesn't look at me. She stares into her coffee like it holds all the answers she is scared to give.

"Talk to me, babe."

"I can't while that's..." she points at my dick, "... staring at me."

London looks up at me, and my lip twitches as she glares.

Yielding to the moment and hoping she will open up to me, I sit beside her on the edge of the bed and drape the sheet over my lap.

After several seconds, London sighs. "I'm doing it for my mom," she finally says, her voice barely above a whisper, filled with emotion. "She has Alzheimer's, and it's an aggressive form that has taken away so much of her in a short time. I had to make the difficult decision to put her in an assisted living facility because it became too challenging to care for her on my own. The costs are staggering..." She sighs. "Much more than I can comfortably manage with my current income at the firm." She takes a moment, her shoulders trembling slightly under the weight of her words, but she forces herself to straighten up. "I needed a simple solution."

I drag a hand down my face. "You should've told me."

London lets out a bitter and shaky laugh. "Told you? I don't belong to you, Kallum. You don't belong to me. So why would I tell you anything?"

Her words sting more than I care to admit, but I ignore the burning sensation deep in my chest they leave behind. "You've been *mine* longer than you care to admit, and you are part of the Kings' family. You have a whole damn support system behind you, but you're too damn stubborn to see it."

"My problems aren't my friends' problems. And I sure as hell don't expect them, or you, to come in and fix my life," London fires back, her voice cracking with indignation. "What would you have done if you'd known? Would you really hand over thousands a month for my mom to get the care she so desperately deserves?"

"I'd pay that and then some without a second thought!"

London's eyes blaze with intensity. "Why? My mom is nothing to you!" I feel the heat of her anger radiating from her body.

"But she means everything to you, babe, and that's all that matters," I retort, frustration consuming me, unable to control the growl that escapes my throat. I stand. "You're not goin' back and takin' your clothes off for another man," I say, calm but firm, knowing I'm throwing kerosene on the fire.

London shoots to her feet. "You don't get a say in what I do."

I tower over her, my body humming with the need to fuck that attitude right out of her. "The fuck I don't."

London glares at me. "Fuck you, Kallum. I. Do. *Not*. Belong. To. You." She pushes against my chest, but I don't budge. I won't let her push me away. She wants to fight, wants to rage, but beneath it all, she is breaking, and I'll be damned if she does it alone.

Without a word, I wrap my arms around her, pulling her tight against me. At first, her body is stiff, locked down, and defiant. She pushes harder, fists pressing against my chest, but I don't let go.

I hold her.

Silent.

Steady.

Solid.

I feel it—the moment she gives in.

Her shoulders slump, and a shudder rips through her body. London presses her head against my chest, and her hands cling to my skin like she hates herself for needing me. The first sob is small and muffled.

The sound cracks me wide open.

I say nothing. I don't ask questions. I don't offer words she doesn't want to hear. I simply let her break apart in my arms. Her tears soak onto my flesh, hot and fast. Her body shakes, her chest rising and falling in uneven breaths as the weight she's been carrying alone finally crushes her.

I fucking hate it.

I hold her tighter, burying my face in her hair, breathing her in.

She cries for a long time until her body has nothing left to give, and I absorb what I can until the storm inside her burns out.

"This doesn't change anything, you know." London breathes in deep.

"The hell it don't."

London pulls back, looking up at me. She opens her mouth to argue, but nothing comes out as I lay her on the bed. Her breathing hitches, and her body stills beneath me. I grip her hips as she lets me settle between her legs. "You're mine."

"I don't need saving." She lifts her hips off the mattress.

"Don't change the fact that you're mine." I slide into her with one hard thrust. "You don't get to push me away," I growl against her ear. "No more fighting."

London whimpers. "I can't afford to stop."

I slide in deeper, dragging a moan from her throat, the kind that makes me fuck her harder. "You can." My voice is rough with possession. "You will."

"I don't need you," she lies, gripping the sheets, her body betraying every stubborn word that leaves her lips.

"You need me," I counter, grinding into her, making her feel how much I need her. "Just as much as I need you." I move faster. "Say it!"

"No," she rasps.

"You belong to me." I grind against her, slow and deep, making her feel every inch of me. "Give me what I want, babe."

Her body tightens, and a strangled moan slips past her lips. And finally, she gives in to me. "I'm yours," she says, her back arching as her orgasm shatters through her body, taking me over the edge of release with her.

I still inside her, pressing my forehead to hers, breathing hard, my pulse pounding. She's boneless beneath me, her body trembling, the fight drained from her once again. I slide my hand down her side, over the curve of her hip, grounding myself in the feel of her. "You're fuckin' perfect."

London sighs, her breath still uneven. "I'm far from perfect. And don't go thinking just because you're a sexy mountain of muscle with a magic dick, it means you're always going to get your way."

I kiss her, chuckling. "That so?"

"Damn right."

I smirk, nipping at her skin, ready to go another round. "I wouldn't want it any other fuckin' way, babe."

We take our time coming down from the high, tangled in each other, until reality slowly creeps back in. Eventually, she slips out of bed and starts getting dressed.

When she turns to me, her eyes lock onto mine with a challenge. "You need to take me home."

I finish pulling my shirt over my head, stepping toward her. "Not happenin'."

Her hands land on her hips, her glare sharpening. "Excuse me?"

I grab my cut from the chair, pulling it on. "I've got shit to handle at the clubhouse, and you're comin' with me."

London folds her arms beneath her breasts. "No, I am *not*. I have a life of my own, Kallum."

I close the space between us in a single stride. "You were abducted last night. If it wasn't for Tony, there's no tellin' what would have happened to you." Dark, unwanted thoughts ripple through my head. "All because you were pokin' around places you shouldn't have been.

London's jaw tightens, and I know she's about to explode. "I was trying to find out what happened to Amara. She was clearly being abused by the asshole she's with, and now she's been missing for days."

My chest tightens with anger. I know London means well, but she put herself in the crosshairs of dangerous men. "You know better," I say, my voice low but controlled. "You've seen firsthand how shit like this plays out. Yet, you still put yourself in the middle of it."

Her eyes blaze. "So, what? I should ignore the fact that a woman is being beaten, and something much worse could have happened to her?"

"I get it, babe. You care. But you're not a goddamn savior. And now, because of your choices, you're stuck to my side until I make damn sure we know who we're dealin' with."

Her lips part, ready to argue more, but I don't give her a chance. "You are gettin' your sweet ass on my bike, and we're goin' to the clubhouse together. End of discussion."

She exhales sharply, her nostrils flaring as we both hold our ground, eyes locked on each other. She can fume all she wants, but she's not winning this one.

Minutes later, we're outside, with the thick humidity of New Orleans pressing in on us.

I throw my leg over the bike and glance at London as she stands, arms crossed, scowling. "Babe." My tone is a warning.

With a look meant to cut like a knife, she steps forward and swings her leg over, gripping my waist.

I smirk. "See? Not so hard."

London mutters something under her breath, but the rumble of my engine drowns it out.

The ride through the city is smooth, the humid air rushing past us as I weave through traffic. London's body molds to mine, her warmth pressing into my back, arms snug around my waist, and her fingers gripping the edges of my cut. And fuck if it doesn't do something to me. It sends a deep, possessive satisfaction through me. And it's not a feeling I'm willing to let go of any time soon.

As we approach the industrial side of the city, the air thickens with the scent of oil and the river. The clubhouse comes into view. The gate opens as we roll up, my brothers' bikes already lined up out front. I park beside Kiwi's ride and cut the engine. London slides off first, adjusting her T-shirt, tossing me a look of pure irritation, and with a sassy sway to her hips, she heads for the door. I shake my head and follow her inside the clubhouse, where Promise is sitting in the common room with Payton and Josie.

"The guys are in the back." Promise's eyes dart between me and her best friend. I smirk, grabbing London by the hand and yanking her into me.

"Kallum—"

I crush my mouth to hers, swallowing whatever smart-ass remark she was about to make. When I pull back, her lips are parted, and her breath is uneven. "Stay put." Before she can argue, I walk away, leaving her with the women watching with amused grins.

As I push through the door into the back room, the others are already waiting. Riggs sits at the head of the table, arms crossed, watching me intently as I find my seat. "How's London holding up?" he inquires.

"She's fired up," I reply.

Riggs laughs. "I bet. I'm sure I speak for everyone when I say it's about damn time you two got your heads out of your asses."

I look around the table, noticing everyone nodding in agreement and rubbing the back of my neck. *Damn, were we that transparent?*

Riggs clears his throat. "Tony caught up with me this morning. He did some digging last night and shared what he knows about the guy who snatched London. We've got a name and an address. His name is Eddie Rollins."

"Where's he hiding?" I ask.

Riggs tosses a slip of paper onto the table, and it circulates among the group. "Rundown neighborhood, gang-controlled. He's got a hold up there," Riggs says, his voice low and tense.

Wick leans in closer, eyes darting around the room. "We need to be vigilant. That area has seen a lot of deaths lately."

"We rollin' out tonight?" Fender asks.

"Our best shot is to move while the sun's high. No way we wanna be caught in the streets once the sun dips unless it's necessary."

I clench my fists, my blood burning with the need to put hands on the bastard who laid a finger on London.

Riggs' gaze sweeps the table. "We don't take unnecessary risks. We don't get sloppy. We get in, get what we came for, and get the fuck out."

Wick nods. "Gangs have eyes everywhere in that neighborhood. The second we roll in, someone's gonna know. We move quickly. Move smart."

Kiwi exhales through his nose. "We got a set-up for the place?"

Riggs leans back in his chair. "Tony didn't have a full layout, just that it's a one-story shack at the end of the dead-end street. Bars on the windows. No cameras, at least not visible. Place is more of a nest than a home." Riggs then focuses his attention on me. "I want him breathin'. For now."

I grip the table's edge, and Riggs notices my building tension.

He looks at me. "I understand this is personal, but keep your head straight."

I hold his gaze. "I know the drill."

He watches me for another beat. "Good." He then turns to Catcher. "Get the van and follow us." Riggs stands. "Cain, Fender, sit this one out. I need eyes and ears here at the clubhouse." There's a beat of silence. Nova and Fender would rather be on the frontline with the rest of us, but neither would argue with Riggs' order. "Let's move," he barks, and we file out of the room.

I slowly approach the door, briefly making eye contact with London before stepping out into the southern heat.

We don't waste time. Within minutes, Catcher is in the van while the rest of us roll out, heading deep into the city's underbelly.

The streets are narrow, lined with abandoned houses, their windows boarded up, and graffiti marking the walls everywhere. We pass women in short skirts with lifeless eyes standing on the corners while drug deals happen in broad daylight. We roll up to a dilapidated house, with the front porch sagging, at the end of a dead-end street.

Riggs signals, and we move in fast, weapons drawn as we rush the house, kicking the door in. Three men, sitting on a dirty sofa in front of a coffee table, bagging drugs, freeze.

Behind us, Wick and Kiwi cover the door while Catcher remains posted inside the van, prepared for trouble should it find us.

My eyes lock onto one of the motherfuckers, laid back, joint in hand, and a massive bruise on the side of his face. I recognize him immediately from the bar and gym. "Rollins," I mutter. His gaze flickers to mine when I speak his name, and the anger simmering inside grows. Does this fucker know who London is to me and the club? If he doesn't, he's sure as hell about to.

He doesn't flinch. "This ain't your side of town, motherfuckers."

"It is now." I step closer, my gun level with his smug expression.

"You know..." He exhales smoke, unfazed by our presence. "A dog that keeps pissing on someone's lawn eventually comes up missing."

My grip tightens, trying like hell not to pull the trigger.

One of his men shifts nervously and attempts to reach for a gun lying on the coffee table.

A gunshot rings out.

The man's body jerks back onto the couch, blood soaking through his shirt, where Riggs put a bullet through his chest. "You two, on your fucking knees," Riggs growls, his tone dangerous. One man rises slowly, his hands up. The motherfucker I want dead remains seated.

The son of a bitch blows smoke and glares between Riggs and me. "I don't kneel for anyone, especially a bunch of bikers thinking they run this city."

"You think this is about your little street game?" Every breath I take feeds the fire burning in my chest.

"Isn't it?" He never takes his beady eyes off me.

"This little visit is about the woman you grabbed last night. *My woman.*"

He smirks. "Ohhh," he drawls. "You mean the feisty dancer with the mouth? She's yours?" Then he chuckles. "Small world." He cocks his head to the side. "She's been sticking her nose in my business, snooping around where she isn't wanted. She needed to be taught a lesson." Rollins grabs his crotch. "Shame things didn't go as planned. I was going to show her what a real man's cock feels like."

I lose my shit.

I reach down, grab the bastard by the throat, and rip him off the couch. I slam his body against the wall and then force-feed the barrel end of my gun down his fucking throat.

"Everest," Riggs warns, his voice sounding distant over the

sound of blood thrumming in my ears as I struggle to keep from pulling the trigger. After a brief battle with myself, I slam the motherfucker to the floor. "A quick death is too good for you."

He coughs. "You have no idea who you are dealing with."

Wick steps in and quickly zip-ties both men's wrists, then slaps duct tape around their heads, covering their mouths.

"Load 'em up and roll out," Riggs barks, and we drag them out the door, toss them into the van, and get the hell out of there.

The ride back to the clubhouse is quick. I keep my eyes sharp as I focus on the sound of my tires eating up asphalt and the low hum of anger simmering in my chest.

When we pull through the clubhouse gate and head toward the back of the property, the sun is high and hot on my back. We head for the shed, which has nothing but concrete walls, a concrete floor, a steel door, and no windows.

No sounds get in.

No screams get out.

Fender unlocks it, swinging the door open, and the thick, hot air escapes.

Catcher backs the van to the entrance.

"Get 'em out," Riggs orders, his voice flat.

I yank open the van doors and snatch Rollins, my woman's abductor, by his hair and haul him out while Nova grabs the second motherfucker. The wiry little fucker twists and kicks, catching Nova in the nuts with a knee, trying to free himself. My brother slams the guy's body so hard against the van that it rattles.

"Son of a bitch," Nova grinds out through clenched teeth, the anger palpable in his voice. He slams the prick's head into the side of the van, each impact reverberating through the air. After a couple of brutal blows, he tosses him onto the ground. Nova delivers a sharp kick to the guy's ribs. He turns away and walks off, leaving the asshole gasping for breath.

Catcher bends down, lifts the guy off the ground, and shoves him into the shed. I follow behind with Rollins.

Inside, the air hangs heavy and oppressive, saturated with the stench of blood that clings stubbornly to the concrete floors and walls. Chains dangle from the ceiling. Tools are lined up against the walls—rusted and well-worn—each one a sinister device, not for fixing things, but for inflicting pain, shattering bones, and breaking men.

Wick grabs the heavy chain from the ceiling and lowers the hook. I push my victim forward while Wick slaps a pair of cuffs onto the dealer's wrists, disregarding the zip ties, and loops the cuffs onto the hook. Kiwi cranks the chains until the guy's arms stretch over his head, leaving his feet nearly dangling off the floor. Rollins groans, low and angry, as the weight of his body causes the cuffs to dig into his flesh.

Catcher forcefully pushes the second dealer into a steel chair, slicing through his restraints, then pulls his arms back and zip ties his wrists again before ripping the tape from his mouth.

I stand in front of the motherfucker I plan to inflict pain on, and my brothers form a circle around us. I roughly rip the tape off his mouth and, with it, parts of his facial hair.

"You kill me, he kills you." His gaze drifts around us. "All of you," he sneers. His eyes fixate on me. "If I'd known the bitch was yours, I'd have put a bullet in the whore's head," he spews, spittle flying.

I wipe his spit from my face, then use his body like a punching bag, landing one brutal blow after another to his midsection until he's left gasping for breath.

His body swings, the chains creaking under his weight as Riggs steps forward, arms crossed over his chest. "Seems your boss has a hard-on for the Kings. Give up his name."

The motherfucker just breathes heavily, then starts laughing and grinning through his pain. "Fuck. You."

Riggs doesn't say a word. He steps aside and nods at me.

I stroll around the room slowly, like a wolf circling his prey, my gaze drifting over the tools, trying to decide which one suits my fancy—pliers, hammers, files, blades, propane torch, saw—

all instruments of persuasion, capable of making a grown man cry and squeal like a stuck pig. The sledgehammer catches my eye. I wrap my hand around the worn handle, its weight comforting. I turn back toward Rollins, who grins like he has a secret. One I hope he thinks is worth dying for.

"You wanna talk?" I ask, my voice low, steady, and controlled.

He barks a laugh, the kind that makes my fists itch. "Go to hell."

"Wrong answer," I mutter, then swing. The sledgehammer connects with a sickening crack against his kneecap, and his body jerks while a scream rips from his throat. I don't hesitate to swing again, only harder this time.

"There's a slim chance I can convince him to make your death quick and less painful," Riggs says, then adds, "If you start talkin', that is."

Rollins' agonizing groan turns into a broken, unhinged laugh. "I told you to watch your back," he croaks, his eyes locking on mine.

I don't say a damn word.

What I want to do is break bones, shatter every inch of him until there's nothing left to recognize. My fingers twitch around the sledgehammer's handle.

I raise my arm to drive the steel into his other knee.

But Riggs steps forward and lifts a hand. "Hold up."

I freeze mid-swing.

Riggs eyes the bastard with a sharp gaze. "You started the mill fire."

It's not a question.

The bastard smirks. "Your clubhouse was my first choice," he spits, his voice full of smugness. "But the mill was more accessible at the time..." he pauses, then says, "Heard there was another fire in the city last night." He smirks.

My jaw locks. The air in the room changes, growing heavier, and the tension amplifies. I glance at Riggs.

He nods once, his mouth a grim line.

The dumb bastard keeps talking. "Your club is in the way, and my boss doesn't like obstacles. You're fucking with his numbers and stirring shit with street-level runners. He doesn't like bikers with reputations that make people nervous. That's his job." He chuckles low and sinister. "So, I sent messages. I hit where it stings."

I roll the sledgehammer onto my shoulder, the weight of it resting against my neck as I circle behind him. Riggs doesn't stop me. I swing low and fast, driving the steelhead into his lower back with a kidney shot. The impact sends his whole body jerking forward with a strangled gasp.

I let the sledgehammer fall to the concrete floor, and Rollins flinches at the sound. I crack my knuckles and step around to face him.

"Who you workin' for?" Riggs growls.

"I'm still not talking," Rollins mutters.

"Good." I slam my fist into his gut, putting all my rage behind it because this is more than extracting information for me.

This asshole put his hands on my woman.

This is personal.

So I bury my fist in his gut again, and the air leaves his lungs with a violent grunt. I follow with several strikes to the ribs until I hear them crack. I hammer into his face next, my knuckles tearing into his flesh. His nose is broken and bent sideways. Blood is everywhere, but I don't stop. I grip the back of his neck and slam my fist into his mouth, feeling his teeth crunch and my knuckles split.

Still, the bastard doesn't scream.

The only sounds he makes are garbled breaths from choking on his blood.

I step back, chest heaving, blood dripping from my hands, mostly his.

Fender walks over and pours water over the bastard's face to keep him from passing out.

Riggs steps forward. "Who do you work for?" he demands. "We can drag this out for days if necessary. Your death is inevitable, but how long it takes depends on you."

Rollins struggles to lift his head but manages to look at Riggs. "You think you are gods in this city. You're not. The Kings are done."

Seeing he needs more persuading, I draw my knife, crouch beside his left leg, and dig into his flesh, sliding the blade behind his kneecap.

A scream rips from his lungs.

The second guy tied to the chair vomits.

Riggs looks at the weak prick. "String him up, too."

The guy struggles, fighting against his restraints as Nova moves to follow orders.

"Wait, wait, wait..." he cries. "If I talk, will you let me leave?"

"You give us what we want, and you can leave." Nova's voice is calm but deadly.

"Velasco," he blurts. "That's who we're running for." The words tumble out of his mouth.

I stand.

The room stills.

The weight of that name settles heavily over us like a thundercloud.

Wick's voice cuts through it. "Velasco is dead."

The guy spilling his guts swallows hard, his eyes cutting to his friend's bloodied, broken body. "Not him. His son. He said the

Kings killed his father, almost destroying the business his father had built for years. He's got men, weapons, and plenty of connections. He says this city is his now."

My stomach turns, rage burning on the inside. I glance back at Rollins. He's barely breathing and bleeding, but he's fucking smiling. "You're about to take your last breath." My hand tightens around the knife's handle. "Got anything to say?"

"He'll come for you. All of you," he spits.

"Let him." I drive the blade into his chest, right into his heart. I twist until the light in his eyes fades like a dying light bulb.

I look at Nova, who turns and raises his gun at our guest with loose lips.

"But..." his eyes widen with fear, "... you said you'd let me leave if I talked." His eyes fall on Riggs, pleading for his life. "*Please.*"

"I said you could leave. I never said how," Riggs states and Nova puts a bullet between the fucker's eyes. He turns and looks at Riggs.

"What's our next move?" Nova asks.

Riggs glances at all of us, then at the door as if he can already see what's coming down the road. "We lock shit down. Club and family. Until further notice."

The silence that follows is deafening with unspoken truths.

These weren't just warning shots.

Velasco didn't merely ignite a fire.

He sparked a goddamn war.

If he wants New Orleans to bleed, he'd better be ready to drown in blood.

Because this time, we won't stop until the entire Velasco bloodline is buried deep beneath our feet.

12

LONDON

Before I even open my eyes, I know Kallum is gone because I don't feel his heat on my back. When we're in bed together, there is never a moment he's not holding me.

Slowly, I open my eyes and look at the empty space beside me. I reach out and grab the pillow where his head was and hug it close to my body. Kallum's scent still lingers on the soft fabric, and I can't help but close my eyes and breathe it in.

The club is on lockdown, so we spent the night at the clubhouse. That also means my avoiding my best friend and the girls is ending. There's no avoiding it. Kallum has made the changes between him and me clear, and he did so in front of everyone when we walked into the clubhouse hand-in-hand. Then he went and made our situation even clearer by kissing me. I'm sure by now the girls know a little about what has transpired in the past twenty-four hours, but they will want to hear the details from my mouth.

Rolling over in bed, I stare up at the ceiling and wonder how Promise will react when I tell her the truth. She'll be pissed, no doubt. Pissed because we don't keep secrets. I can handle her being mad, though. Her disappointment in me is something I won't be able to take. Either way, it's time to face the music and let the cards fall where they may.

When I walk downstairs, it's still early. The sun isn't up, and since Promise and I won't be going into the office today, she'll take advantage and sleep as long as Jaxson lets her. On the other hand, I have too much on my mind to sleep.

The common room is empty, so I head to the kitchen for a much-needed coffee. When I walk in, Catcher is there, back resting against the counter, a cup of coffee in his hand. "Hey, Catcher."

"Mornin'," he grunts.

Obviously not a morning person.

"You wouldn't happen to know where Kallum is, would you?" I ask.

Catcher downs the last of his coffee and then sets the mug in the sink. "The guys had some shit to look into, said they'd be back by lunch."

By 'shit to do' he means club business. Club business means none of mine. I don't take offense to Catcher's lack of information. I've been around long enough to know the rules of the club. I also know 'said business' is likely to do with my failed kidnapping. "Gotcha." I nod, making my way over to the coffee pot.

"You doin' all right this mornin'?" Catcher asks, catching me off guard. Catcher has been around the club for a while, and though I don't know him well, I do know the man is not one for small talk.

I shrug. "I'm okay. I've never been stun-gunned and kidnapped before. "Ten out of ten, I don't recommend." I try to make light of the situation, but the way Catcher clenches his jaw says he doesn't find my comment amusing.

Sighing, I plop down in a chair at the kitchen table. "Sorry, bad joke. The truth is, it scared the hell out of me, and I'm freaked out. I'm also scared for my friend who is missing."

Catcher's angry expression softens a little at my confession. "We all have our own ways of dealing with bad shit."

"You say that like you're speaking from experience." As soon as I voice my observation, I see Catcher's wall go up. The man is clearly dealing with his own demons. I'm smart enough to know not to push, so I change the subject. Standing, I take my cup with me. "I'm going to get some fresh air. If Promise wakes up and is looking for me, will you tell her where I'm at?"

"Sure." Catcher nods. "Don't wander too far."

I smile. "I won't."

Once outside, I make my way over to the covered veranda and take a seat on the porch swing, tucking my feet under my butt. The sun is just rising over the river, painting the sky in a pretty shade of pink and the promise of a beautiful day. Moments like this remind me of all the mornings I'd wake up and find my mom sitting in our backyard with her cup of coffee as she watched the sunrise. I remember climbing into her lap as a little girl, sleepy-eyed and clueless about all the world's dangers. And not twenty-four hours ago, that danger touched me. I wasn't lying to Catcher when I said it scared the hell out of me. I keep replaying what happened each time I think about the outcome if Tony had not been there.

Kallum was right.

I was reckless.

My recklessness and keeping secrets almost got me killed.

I'm drawn out of my racing thoughts when there is a shuffling sound behind me. I peer over my shoulder at Promise, still clad in her pajamas, and a bright-eyed Jaxon clung to her hip. Her son truly is his father made over. Jaxon has dark hair with a hint of mischief hidden behind his crooked smile. As Promise passes in front of me, I grab Jaxson's little foot. "Good morning, little man."

Promise sets Jaxon at the small kiddie table beside the swing and hands him a sippy cup of milk and a sandwich bag full of dry cereal.

"You're up early," I remark.

"I had to call Zara and tell her I wouldn't be in today. I asked her to reschedule our appointments and take the next few days off."

"Thanks," I mutter. "You know, over the years, I've kind of gotten used to club drama and the occasional lockdown. I just didn't ever expect it would one day be because of me." I try to joke.

Promise doesn't respond. Instead, she remains silent. I take it as a bad sign.

When I can't take the uncomfortable silence, I close my eyes and let the words I've held in for so long tumble out. "I've been stripping at the Pink Paradise for the past three months."

"What?" Promise breathes.

I tip my head to the side to look at the disbelief on her face.

"What... why?" she asks.

"I had no choice," I tell her softly. "Mom's insurance wouldn't cover the cost of her stay at Golden Hills, and there was no way I could let her live elsewhere. I tried to get a night job at a few other places, but it wasn't enough," I tell her. "I did what I had to do."

Promise turns toward me. "London, why didn't you come to me? You know I would have helped."

It kills me to see how truly hurt Promise is that I didn't come to her for help. "You go to your best friend when you need to borrow twenty bucks, Promise, not fifteen thousand. And that's per month. Our firm does well, but not enough that I can keep up the cost every single month."

"London—" Promise goes to argue, but I cut her off.

"I did what I had to do to take care of my mom, Promise. My mom means the world to me and has given me the world. So, if I have to show my tits and dance for the entire state of Louisiana to ensure she gets the best care there is, then that's what I'm going to do." A tear slides down my cheek as I look at my best friend. "My momma is everything to me, Promise."

"Oh, Lon." Promise wraps her arms around me. "I know what your mom means to you. I only wish you'd come to me. You're more than my best friend, you're like a sister. You shouldn't be going through this alone."

I break away from Promise and wipe my cheek with the back of my hand. "That's not the kind of burden you pawn off on your best friend, Promise."

"Pawn off?" Promise looks affronted. "London, is that how you see it? Let me ask you this. If the roles were reversed, would you want me to come to you, or would you want me to suffer alone in silence?"

"Of course, I'd want you to come to me," I say. "But—"

This time, Promise cuts me off. "But nothing. If you're in trouble, the rules are to go to your best friend for help."

"So, there are rules now?" I grin.

"It's an unwritten rule, and you know it." Promise juts out her chin.

"Fine. The next time I'm in trouble, I'll come to you."

"Good. And you're going to let me help with your mom."

I shake my head. "No. I can't let you do that."

"London, there is no way I'm going to let you keep stripping when I have the means to help."

"I love you, Promise, but it's not happening. Besides..." I shrug. "Dancing is not that bad. I love my boss and the girls I work with. I've made some good friends at the Pink Palace."

I can tell Promise is skeptical. "You mean, you want to keep dancing?"

"No, but it's a sacrifice I'm willing to make to help my mom. I'm just saying the people I work with make it possible."

"What's Everest say?" Promise asks.

"Kallum doesn't have a say in what I do."

Promise bites her bottom lip to try to hide her smile. "We'll see."

I roll my eyes. "We'll see my ass. I'm not letting any man tell me what I can and can't do."

At that, Promise lets out a full-on cackle. "Oh, London. You have so much to learn when it comes to these men. I have a feeling you will find out sooner rather than later, though."

"Please, I can handle Kallum."

Promise doesn't look convinced. "Whatever you say, London. I can tell you now that my money is on Everest. There is no way he's letting you back on that stage. When one of these men claims a woman, they are claimed."

"You make them sound like cavemen?"

"That's because they are." Promise giggles. "You have been around long enough to see that it's true. Only now, it's your turn to experience it. And I have to say, it's been a long time coming, that's for sure."

"What are you on about now?"

Promise makes a tsking sound. "Don't be dense. Everyone has been watching you and Everest dance around each other since the day you met. I'm just surprised it took y'all this long to get your shit together. I bet the sex was off the charts with all the back-and-forth flirting that's been happening. The sexual tension has been off the charts."

My mouth hangs open at her bold observation. "How do you know we had sex?"

Promise looks at me like I've grown a second head. "Hello, a woman can tell when her best friend has been laid... and laid good and proper. And you, London, have most definitely been laid." Promise leans into me, her expression serious. "I have to know. How was it?"

I want to stay irritated with my best friend, but the truth is, I can't. Half the fun of having a best friend is talking about men. "Best I ever had. Bar none," I confess.

Promise's face lights up with a huge grin. "I'm happy for you."

I laugh. "You're happy I'm having good sex?"

"Ah, yeah. Rules are if your best friend is having the best sex of her life, you're happy for her," Promise says with mock irritation.

"Best sex of your life?" a deep voice rumbles.

Startled, I turn to see Everest standing just inside the door, looking as smug as ever.

I narrow my eyes on him. "What makes you think I was talking about you?"

His lip twitches like he's trying not to laugh. The bastard knows I was talking about him.

"What are you doing eavesdropping anyway? Catcher said you wouldn't be back until later."

Everest stalks toward me, carrying a paper bag with a familiar logo and a cup filled with what I already know will be my favorite coffee. "I stopped at that coffee shop down the street from your apartment and got that sugary shit you call coffee and one of those blueberry muffins you like."

I gape at him. "How did you know?"

Everest sets my muffin and coffee on the table in front of me and leans down until his face is level with mine. "I pay attention."

"Really?" I whisper.

"Yes," he whispers back. "Now, give me a kiss because I got shit to do." Without waiting for a response, Everest claims my mouth with his. The kiss is quick but no less toe-curling. A second later, his mouth is gone, and so is he.

Once I know we are alone, I turn back to Promise, who is fighting her own grin. I roll my eyes. "Shut up."

She holds up her hands. "Hey! I didn't say a word."

I snatch the bag off the table and retrieve the muffin from inside. "No, but I know what you were thinking."

Promise reaches over, tears off a piece of my muffin, and pops it in her mouth. "You have been giving me a hard time for years. Now it's finally my turn."

Later that afternoon, I'm lounging around the clubhouse with the girls. Because we are on lockdown and there's nothing else to do, we make margaritas and gossip while Jo's daughter, Sawyer, and Tequila's niece, Sydney, watch the little kids in the television room. At the same time, poor Catcher is sitting in the corner of the room, looking like he'd rather be elsewhere. I don't blame him. No man should bear witness to the kinds of things girlfriends say when they are bored and have been drinking.

"I don't care what anyone says, strippers are hot," Tequila says, sprawled out on the sofa, putting her two cents in. "I always did want to learn how to pole dance, but unfortunately, these feet were made for boots, not stilettos."

I wave her off. "Anyone can learn. I'll be happy to teach you some moves."

Piper perks up. "Ooh, can you teach me too?"

"Wait." Luna signs. "I want to learn too."

"Don't forget about me," Jo adds.

"Hell, yeah." I raise my drink in the air. "I vote that next girls' night should be at the Pink Palace. I'll introduce you guys to Tony and the girls."

There is a round of cheers from the girls just as the guys walk into the clubhouse.

"Awe, shit. They're into the margaritas," Wick drawls. "That can only mean one thing."

In the corner, Catcher murmurs, "You don't want to know."

Promise giggles when Nova strides up behind her and tugs her ponytail, making her head tip back. "What are you all up to?"

Over on the sofa, Tequila pretends to inspect her nails. Across from her, Luna's face turns red, and Piper bites her bottom lip beside Luna as Kiwi eyes her skeptically.

"What makes you think we're up to something?" I tease Nova with a smirk.

Beside him, Everest crosses his arms over his broad chest. "Maybe because every time you women get together, one of you gets a hair-brained idea to do something stupid, and the rest of you fall in line."

"No. What happens is we try to have fun, and then you all come in with your caveman attitudes and spoil it," I argue.

Lucky for us, Riggs cuts in. "All right, brothers. We got shit to do, so whatever the women are cookin' up, we'll have to deal with it later." I watch as Riggs strides over to Luna and steals a kiss before disappearing out the back with Fender and Wick.

"Pain in my goddamn ass," Everest grunts, then stalks off with Kiwi and Nova.

13

EVEREST

The light cutting through the curtains is dull and gray, filtered by storm clouds hanging low in the sky. Fitting for the shitstorm circling us. I've been lying awake for a couple of hours, the weight of the past few days pressing heavily on my chest. I look to my left, where London is curled on her side, one bare leg half tangled in the sheet, with her long dark hair a mess on the pillow. Peaceful. Safe. For now.

We're on lockdown, thanks to Velasco. Not the one we buried a few years back, but his son. The one who decided to crawl out of whatever hole he'd been hiding in to make us pay for the blood we spilled. And if there's one thing I know, it is that people seeking revenge don't care about right or wrong. Organizations like Velasco's care about legacy and power. This new blood is looking to restore what was lost. And now that we know the pusher who tried to take London was connected to Velasco, it's all starting to stack up.

But something tells me it's not that simple.

This young woman London worked with at the club, Amara, is the reason my woman went snooping around in the first place. So, there was no connection between London being taken and the Velasco shit. Rollins' interest in my woman was purely his own. The two separate situations just happened to intertwine.

I stare at the ceiling, piecing it all together again like a damn crime board. Now, not only do we have a target on our backs, with Velasco wanting us out of the picture, but this young woman, Amara, is still missing.

London stirs, and a wispy breath slips past her lips. Her eyes open. "Hey," she murmurs.

"Sleep all right?"

London stretches. "As well as I can."

I nod and slide up to lean against the headboard.

"You didn't sleep?" London eyes me.

"Not much. Been thinkin'."

"About?"

"Everything. The person who hurt you, the trouble haunting the club, us," I admit, as it continues to swirl in my mind.

London sits up, pulling the sheets with her. "I need to find Amara."

I hear the worry and concern in her voice, but I'll be damned if we have a repeat of what happened the first time she went rogue, looking for the young woman on her own.

I clench my jaw. "I know you are concerned, babe, but don't get it in that pretty little head that you can do somethin' about it," I warn her. "That fucker might very well be connected to Amara's disappearance, but his ties to that situation and you snoopin' around is only half of it. He was part of a bigger threat, not just to Amara or you, but to the club. That asshole crossed both our paths. They may not be the same stories, but they're twisted together." I exhale hard, wound tight with building tension.

London leans over, trailing her fingernails down my abs. "I don't want to think right now." Her lips touch mine, soft and sweet, then hungry.

I grab the back of her head, deepening the kiss, and pull her into my lap. The sheet drops, and her bare skin meets mine, and all rational thought flies the fuck out the window.

I wanted her from the moment she walked into our lives. But now? It's much more than want. It's need. It's possession. She's *mine*. Every inch of her, every breath, every fucking heartbeat.

"Fuck," I mutter against her as she reaches between us and strokes my cock. "You got no idea what you do to me." I dip my head, taking one of her nipples into my mouth, and London gasps.

"Then show me."

Just as I flip her under me, ready to do just that...

Bang. Bang. Bang.

"Everest." Fender's voice is outside the door. "Prez is callin' church. *Now*."

I groan, pressing my forehead to London's, my dick throbbing, ready to sink into her pussy. "Motherfucker's got the worst timing."

London laughs softly while reaching between us, grabbing my dick and teasingly rubbing the head up and down her slit, then stroking it against her clit. And fuck if I don't damn near come right then and there, watching her. She moans, then says, "Rain check?"

I growl, giving her one last kiss, rough and deep. "This ain't over, babe."

She smiles. "Damn right it's not."

By the time I pull on my jeans and boots, I've managed to cool down enough for my dick to do the same. I cast one last glance at London, her hair wild and eyes stormy, her lips swollen from our kiss. The look she gives me says she is just as frustrated that we don't get to finish what we started.

Sighing, I head downstairs, where the smell of coffee hangs heavy in the air. I grab a cup of caffeine and head toward the back of the building, where my brothers sit around the table. Like always, Riggs is at the head, with Wick beside him. I sit across from Kiwi, whose laptop is open, fingers flying across the keys. Nova leans back in his chair, sipping his coffee, and Fender does the same, all looking tired.

The door closes, and Riggs gets to business. "Let's get started." He sighs. "Here's what we know. Velasco's son is gunnin' for us. And word is spreadin' that he wants vengeance."

Wick leans forward. "The streets are talkin', saying he's got one of the local gangs backin' him."

I put my elbows on the table. "We also got a missin' woman, Amara. The one London was lookin' for. We can't ignore the connection between the dead motherfucker who attempted to shut London up and Velasco. The former Velasco didn't just run drugs, he was runnin' in the skin trade too." My gut coils at the thought of what could have happened to London if Tony hadn't reacted in time as he did.

"Fuck," Riggs states.

"So, what's the play?" Nova asks.

Riggs glances around the table. "We lock it down tighter than a gnat's ass. No one goes solo. Women stay close. We ride only if we have to. I want someone with the women full-time. Keep eyes on our families." His eyes cut to Kiwi. "Kiwi, keep diggin'. I want a face, location, and anything we can find on this new Velasco. Y'all see somethin' I'm the first to know. Got it?" Riggs' tone is stern, all business. He stands. "I know we all got shit to do and lives to live. Roll out and stay vigilant."

With church over, I set out to find Catcher. I have something to handle and need his help. I find him in the kitchen, drinking coffee and sitting alone. He looks at me. "Need you with London. Don't let her out of your sight. Tell her to take it up with me if she gets pissy."

He nods. "Roger that."

I step into the main room of the clubhouse. It's quieter than usual but not dead. Everyone is mingling, staying close for now while tending to the kids. Over by the pool table, I spot Nova. He has his arm draped casually over Promise's shoulder, head bent low, saying something only she's meant to hear, judging by the blush on her cheeks. Piper is near them, perched on the arm of the sofa, with Kiwi's arm around her waist. I walk up to Nova, nodding. "Need to go handle somethin'. Mind ridin' along?"

Nova leans in and kisses Promise without questioning me, then turns to Piper and presses a quick kiss to the side of her head. He then looks at Kiwi. "Keep them safe."

"You got it." Kiwi salutes.

Nova follows me through the front door. There's no sun today, but the air is thick and muggy. I head for the bikes, and as we walk, Nova glances sideways at me.

"So, you and London."

"Yup."

"About time you two finally stopped pretendin' you didn't want to take a bite," he says, swinging a leg over his bike.

I chuckle low and rough. "We're still navigatin' what we got or where it's goin'. But I'm in it, brother. For however long, or whatever comes our way, I'm here for the ride," I confess.

Nova nods. "That's all that fuckin' matters."

I climb onto my bike, the rumble of the engine resonating under my grip as I twist the throttle. Nova follows suit, his bike roaring to life beside me, and we roll out onto the road together.

The ride out to the facility is quiet. Nova and I cruise side by side down a long stretch of a two-lane highway. The further we get from town, the more my mind drifts. Not to Velasco or the threat hanging over our heads. London consumes my headspace. We're moving fast. Fast enough to rattle a man who doesn't rattle easily. But when you know, you know. And I do. Without a doubt, when I picture my future, London is the center of it.

We pull into the parking lot of the nursing home. It's quaint, tucked away behind a line of pine trees. It's damn near peaceful.

Nova kills his engine, eyeing me, looking for answers.

"London's mom is here," I offer, and he nods.

"I'll keep post out here." Nova climbs off his bike and stretches his legs.

Inside, I handle one of the things I came for—money. London won't need to stress about her mom's care again. Before I go, I ask if I can see her.

The nurse who leads me down the hall to Faye's room smiles. "She's having a really good day." We stop outside room 208.

When I step into the room, I stop cold. Faye is sitting by the window. The sun finally breaks through the dark clouds, spilling over her hair as she lifts a mug to her lips. She turns and sees me standing in the doorway. Faye looks like my woman—older, softer, but with the same eyes.

"You must be Everest," she says, her voice sweet and steady. "I would know you anywhere by how my girl talks about you."

"Yes, ma'am. That's me," I say, and walk into the room, sitting in an empty chair across from her. "She talks about me, huh?" I can't help but grin.

Faye laughs softly. "All the time."

"I care about her," I admit.

Faye looks out the window, her gaze far off like she's seeing memories she doesn't want to let go of. "London was always a strong one. As a child, she always insisted on standing on her own two feet, even when they were shaking."

That's my woman.

Faye turns back to me, and her eyes, like London's, lock onto mine with startling clarity. "You know she's scared, right? Not of you. But of what it means to need someone. To lean on someone. It's just not in her nature, but she wants it nonetheless. With you."

I nod but remain quiet because I feel she has more to say.

"My daughter needs someone who won't buckle. Someone who will be her peace when the world is on fire and her strength when hers runs out." She places her hand on top of mine. "There will come a day when I won't be here anymore. And I don't just mean the breathing part. This disease I have, it's a thief, Everest, stealing pieces of me every day, little by little. And one day, it will take the rest. I won't remember her name or her face. But my baby will remember the pain. She'll carry it for the rest of her life."

My throat tightens—the weight of her words anchoring in my chest like concrete.

"She's gonna need someone who doesn't just love her, but someone who stays." She pauses. "Promise me you'll be that man. That you will be her strength when everything else falls apart."

I squeeze her hand. "I promise to be all that and more. Whatever she needs, whatever it takes, I'll be that man."

A tear slides down her cheek, and she nods. "Then I can let go of some of this worry. I can see that you will burn the world down for her." There's another silence before Faye says, "She loves you. I may forget sometimes, but I'll never forget the light in her eyes when she says your name. That kind of light doesn't lie."

My jaw clenches as I fight back a wave of emotions tightening in my chest.

Faye leans back in her chair, a tired smile lingering on her lips. We sit in silence for a few more moments before I finally rise to leave.

She reaches for my hand again. "Don't let her push you away when she's scared. My girl's heart is bigger than she will ever admit."

I lean down and kiss the top of her head. "I won't."

I leave with more weight on my chest than before stepping foot in this place, making a vow to a woman who won't remember my name one day. But she will never forget what love looks like when she sees me and London together.

Since we're already out this way, I decide to swing in at Pink

Paradise and see Tony. I lift a hand signaling to Nova, and he pulls in behind me.

We park out front. The place is quiet. There are no cars because the doors haven't opened yet, and we cut the engines.

"What's up?" Nova asks.

"Thought we'd check in with Tony, see if he's got anything on Velasco." I climb off my bike.

Nova scans our surroundings and then looks toward the entrance of the club. "Feels wrong."

He ain't the only one sensing something is off.

Before going in, we head around back, checking shit out. It smells like piss and beer soured by the heat. The dumpster's lid is half open, and crushed beer and whiskey bottles are scattered everywhere. I reach for the back door's handle. It's unlocked. I look at Nova. That's our first red flag.

We take out our weapons, keeping them at our sides, walk inside, and make our way to the front of the building. The air is thick, and it's too damn quiet. We move slowly as broken glass crunches beneath our boots. The place looks like a tornado ripped through it, broken bottles, chairs overturned, and tables flipped.

"The place is torn the fuck up," Nova mutters, looking around.

He strolls over, flicking switches on the wall. "Lights are dead."

We move across the room and enter the hallway.

My gut twists. "You smell that?"

"Yeah," Nova whispers. "Blood."

A low, pained grunt coming from the back breaks the silence.

We raise our guns and move toward the sound. We pass the girls' dressing room, trashed just like the rest of the place.

We reach the office, the door half off its hinges. Inside, we find Tony slumped in his chair behind the desk, his shirt soaked in blood and one arm hanging limp at his side. His face is wrecked, one eye swollen shut, his lip split down the middle, and blood dripping from his nose.

"Fuck," I mutter, holstering my weapon. "Tony."

His head jerks up, barely.

Nova moves in fast, crouching beside the old man. "What the hell happened?"

Tony coughs, wincing. "Velasco. He sent two of his goons in here. Tore the place up, then did the same to me."

"You know the name Velasco?" I ask, hoping he'll have more intel than we do.

Tony shakes his head. "First I've heard of it, but I sure as shit know it now, and I'm fuckin' pissed." His fingers dig into the chair's armrest, his knuckles turning white as he tries to stand but fails. "This got anything to do with London or Amara's disappearance?"

I shake my head. "No. This is aimed at the Kings."

Nova pulls out his phone and steps away. "Callin' Prez." He speaks low and fast, giving a rundown of the situation, then comes back. "Prez says, get him to the clubhouse."

Tony waves him off. "Fuck that. I'm not leaving my place."

"You just got your ass handed to you, old man," I growl. "You need patchin' up."

"I'll heal," he says, spitting blood to the side. "But what I won't do is run."

Nova doesn't argue. He pulls his phone out. "I'm callin' Teagan."

A stretch of time passes with nothing but Tony's labored breaths filling the space.

When Teagan arrives, she looks around but doesn't ask questions. She mutters, "Jesus," under her breath. Moving fast, she gets to work. "Stay still," she says, opening a gauze pack. Tony doesn't even flinch as she cleans the gash on his temple. Once Teagan is done and Tony is patched up, she places a bottle of pills on his desk. "Nothing appears to be broken, but that doesn't mean there aren't fractures. You should have X-rays done to rule it out."

Tony groans, adjusting himself in the chair. "I'm all right. Appreciate the house call, though."

Teagan reaches into her bag. "This should knock the edge off for a few hours. If you want more, you'll have to get it yourself." She then turns to Nova and me. "I'll see myself out."

"Give us a minute, and we'll follow you back to town. Not risking your safety after doin' us a favor," Nova says.

She sighs but doesn't argue.

I look at Tony. "You sure you wanna stay? They could come back."

Tony leans over and opens the bottom drawer of his desk. From inside, he pulls out a monster of a revolver, matte black steel, and a long barrel with six chambers. "Dirty Harry style," he mutters. "They caught me off-guard, but if those motherfuckers come back, I'll be the one putting them in the ground."

"You're not alone on this, old man. The club has your back," I say.

Tony locks eyes with me. "I know. But let the record show, if this Velasco motherfucker wants to start a war with me, he's got one." He rests the revolver on his desk, keeping his hand on the grip.

14

LONDON

We've been on lockdown here at the clubhouse for a few days, and it doesn't appear the guys are any closer to finding out who this Velasco character is. The club feels that as long as he's out in the streets of New Orleans, I'm not safe, which doesn't exactly give me a warm, fuzzy feeling. The guy already sent one of his goons to kidnap me, so who's to say he won't succeed the second time?

In a perfect world, I want to believe Amara came to the realization she wasn't safe and got the hell out of town, but I know that's not the case. She would have at least told Tony of her plans if that were true.

Being cooped up in the clubhouse day after day doesn't help my wandering thoughts either. Luckily, Promise and I were able to convince the guys to let us go to the office today. We can only put off our clients for so long. Promise and I have several court dates approaching, and there is no way I'm allowing my clients to suffer because my personal life is currently a shit show. Returning to work, however, did come with stipulations. One, we don't go anywhere without Catcher. He is now our shadow. And two, we don't go anywhere but to the office. That means no lunch date with friends and no visiting my mom. That last condition had me up in arms until Riggs explained how visiting my mom might bring danger to her doorstep. I had to admit he was right, but I felt like an idiot because I hadn't thought of that. Then I had a whole panic attack, questioning if Velasco already knew about my mom and if he'd do something to hurt her to get to me. Riggs assured me he had someone watching my mom to ease my mind. He gave me his word that nothing would harm her.

"Babe," Kallum calls out, snapping me back to the present. I realize I've been spaced out in front of the mirror for several minutes in nothing but my bra and underwear. I hadn't even realized he'd taken a shower.

"You say something?" I ask.

"I asked if you knew when you'd be done today."

"I'm not sure. I have to play catch-up, so it's probably late. Why?"

Kallum comes up behind me and wraps an arm around my waist, pulling my back flush against his chest. He kisses my neck, sending shivers down my spine. "I was thinking I'd pick you up and take you to dinner."

I tip my head back and meet his eyes. "I'd like that."

Kallum steals a kiss, and his hand starts to creep into the waistband of my panties. "Oh no, you don't," I mumble into his mouth. "I have to leave in five minutes, and Promise is probably downstairs waiting on me."

"She can wait." Kallum nips at my bottom lip.

"I'm not doing that to her, it's rude."

"Rude is makin' me walk around all day with my dick hard."

"You'll live." I shove him with my elbow. "Besides, my first meeting is in twenty minutes. We don't have time."

Kallum gives up his quest, but not without grumbling.

After putting on a dark gray pencil skirt and blouse, I sit down on the edge of the bed and slide on a pair of slingback heels. "I'll make it up to you tonight."

"Fuck yeah, you will." Everest pulls his cut over his shoulders. "Tonight, you're going to put that mouth to some other use besides pissin' me off."

"Hey, I make no promises. The day has just begun. There's plenty of time to figure out how to make you mad."

By lunchtime, Promise and I are rethinking whether the fuss we made was worth coming into the office. When we first arrived at the office, Catcher perched himself outside the entrance before we made him sit in a corner in our small waiting room. We learned quickly that a huge, broody biker standing guard in front of the building might not be good for business. Promise's first client of the day was Mrs. Dexter. Catcher's presence scared the hell out of her. Mrs. Dexter is a sweet eighty-two-year-old woman whose husband passed away last year. She had been married to the late Mr. Dexter for over forty-seven years. They had two daughters together, and Mr. Dexter has a son from a previous relationship.

It turns out that his son didn't take too kindly to his father, leaving his wife and two daughters with everything in his will. The point is that his good-for-nothing son had robbed them blindly after he hooked up with some bad people when he was twenty-one and then left town. Mrs. Dexter said he'd show up every few years with some sob story about losing his job or apartment.

They'd let him come home and try to help get him on a straight path, but then he'd just disappear in the middle of the night, taking anything of value with him. They hadn't seen or heard from him in close to ten years. Then he heard about his father's passing, and suddenly, he was back in town. Let's just say he was expecting to hit it big and was sorely disappointed when his stepmother and sisters got everything. We're talking two point two million dollars. Poor Mrs. Dexter and her daughters have fought her stepson for eight months. Luckily, they are due in court in a few weeks. Promise has that case in the bag, though. Mrs. Dexter will come out on top when it's all said and done.

Exiting my office, I see Promise at the entrance, saying goodbye to Mrs. Dexter. "I don't know about you all, but I'm starved." I look at Catcher. "You good with pizza?"

"Pepperoni and sausage, no olives." He grunts.

"Noted." I turn to Zara, who is sitting at her desk. "What about you?"

"I'm not fussy. I'll eat whatever you guys get."

"Cool." I pull out my cell, dial the pizza place down the block, and order delivery. "Pizza will be here in twenty minutes," I tell Promise once she's done seeing Mrs. Dexter off. "I'm going to call and check on my mom. Let me know when the food is here," I call out over my shoulder on my way back to my office.

Sitting behind my desk, I use my laptop to pull up my bank account to ensure I have sufficient funds to make this month's payment at Golden Hills. Once I ensure all is in order, I call the director, Mr. Briggs, who answers on the third ring.

"Good afternoon, Mr. Walker. This is Ms. Monroe."

"Hello, Ms. Monroe. How are you?"

"I'm well. I'm just calling to see if I can settle my mother's bill over the phone and to ask how she is doing. Unfortunately, I can't get there to see her today."

"I looked in on Faye this morning, and she's doing great. If you like, I can have her nurse call you later this afternoon with an update."

"That would be great."

"Oh, it's no problem at all. Anything to help. As for the matter of your mother's bill, it's been settled."

Confused, I ask, "Settled? What do you mean? I haven't paid yet."

"I'm sorry, Ms. Monroe, I thought you were aware."

"No, I wasn't. Can you tell me who paid it?" I ask, but I already have my suspicions.

"Sure, let me just pull up your mom's file." I hear the shuffling of papers over the phone. "Here it is. It says it was settled with Mr. Mercer. He is a really nice gentleman. He stopped by yesterday. He ordered all transactions associated with your mother's stay to be drafted from his bank account indefinitely."

That asshole.

When I don't say anything, Mr. Walker says, "Ms. Monroe, are you there?"

"Yes, I'm here. Sorry about that. Thank you so much for your help."

"You're welcome, Ms. Monroe. And I'll be sure to have your mother's nurse call you soon."

I end the call and immediately dial Kallum's number.

He answers on the first ring. "Babe."

I'm fuming by this point and barely allow him to get that one word out before I lay into him. "The next time you decide to take it upon yourself and butt into my life where my mom is concerned, you might want to consider asking me how I feel about it."

"London, calm down."

"I will *not* calm down. You had *no right*. And as soon as I'm able to, I'll be going down to Golden Hills and fixing everything."

"London," Kallum growls, but I hang up before he can say another word. Two seconds later, he tries calling me back. I stare at his name flashing on the screen before declining the call and placing my cell on Do Not Disturb.

Promise pokes her head into my office. "Hey, pizza is here."

I fix my face and smile. "Okay."

Sensing something is wrong, she asks, "You good? Is it your mom?"

"No, Mom is good. Everything is fine. I'm just hungry." I start to follow Promise down the hall when the sound of rumbling pipes stops me in my tracks. *Shit!*

Catcher stands from his corner on high alert as Kallum storms through the entrance, his eyes trained on me, and he not only looks mad, he's fucking fuming.

"What's going on?" Promise asks.

Instead of answering, Kallum storms past Promise and doesn't stop as he grabs my arm and drags me back down the hall.

"What the hell?" I try pulling free of his hold.

Kallum kicks the door shut with his foot when we get to my office. "You want to explain what the hell that call was about?" he barks.

"I'm pretty sure I made myself clear when we spoke."

"Correction, London. We didn't do anything. That was all you. You didn't shut your mouth long enough to let me get a word in edgewise."

I cross my arms over my chest. "Are you seriously going to barge in here and get mad at me when it was you who overstepped?"

"It's not overstepping when I see my woman struggling to keep her head above water, and I do what needs to be done to make sure she can breathe more easily."

"Without discussing with me whether or not that's what I wanted?" I counter. "I don't need you stepping in like some knight in shining armor, Kallum. I'm perfectly capable of taking care of my mother on my own. I have a job that pays me enough to do so."

"And I said no woman of mine was goin' to be showin' her tits for other men." Kallum's face turns red.

"Yeah, I heard you, Kallum, but I didn't agree."

Kallum takes a step forward, pinning me against my desk. "I don't need you to agree because that's what it is. I know we are getting to know each other, but let me help you out by being perfectly clear, I'm not the kind of man who sees his woman struggling and doesn't move mountains to make her road less bumpy. I'm the kind of man who, when his woman cries in his arms because she hasn't been able to breathe easy in a long fuckin' time, shelters some of her burdens so that she can sleep better at night." Kallum leans in close to my face, his chest heaving. "And I'm damn sure not the kind of man who is okay with his woman showing parts of her body that are meant for me and me alone."

"I...umm," I stammer. "That's a lot to take in."

"You'll deal! Let that shit sink in, and then we'll move on." Then his face turns soft as he grips the back of my neck. "But I also know the kind of woman you are, and what I didn't know, I'm learning. I know you're a woman who is strong and independent. So, when someone challenges your independence, it makes you feel less than and throws you off-balance. Just know that was not my intention. From now on, I'll be mindful of that fact and come talk to you beforehand." He finishes with, "Especially when it comes to your mom," which leaves me speechless. And surprisingly, a lot turned on.

Sensing the change, Kallum's pupils dilate. My breathing becomes labored when his palm slides from the back of my neck down the front of my blouse over my rapidly beating heart. There is a beat of silence between us. The next thing I know, my shirt is ripped open, and my bra cups are shoved down. I cry out when Kallum's mouth latches onto one of my nipples while I expertly work at unbuttoning his jeans. I'm just about to slip my hand down the front of his boxer briefs when suddenly, I'm spun around, face forward against my desk. Cold air hits my backside as my skirt is shoved up around my hips. My panties are tugged to the side and replaced with the tip of Kallum's cock.

"Fuckin' soaked," he hisses as he teases my entrance.

"Stop teasing and fuck me already," I snap.

There is no mistake about the glint in Kallum's eyes when I peer back at him. "I'm going to like fightin' with you," he confesses just before slamming into me. "Your smart mouth is the sexiest thing about you."

My breath catches in my throat as I fight like crazy, not to make a sound. Behind me, Kallum shows no mercy while he drills into me. "Don't stop," I beg.

Kallum's fingers dig into my hips, and there is no doubt he will leave his mark. When I confessed he was the best I've ever had, I wasn't lying. No man has ever come close to satisfying or filling me the way Kallum does.

He was made just for me.

"I'm close," I pant the second my orgasm starts to build. As soon as the words slip past my lips, Kallum lets go of my hips. One arm curls around my belly, lifting me off the desk and flush against his chest while his hand wraps around the front of my neck. The hand on my neck constricts as he growls into my ear. "Be a good girl and come for me." His command is my undoing. On instinct, I seek out his mouth. Kallum wastes no time giving me what I crave, and I cry into his mouth as my orgasm crashes through me.

15

EVEREST

Outside, the sun is long gone, and inside, the clubhouse is filled with the low hum of the women unwinding after getting kids settled while we men hash out intel over a cold beer. We've been at this table for hours, running down every name, location, and rumor tied to Velasco, and we still have nothing solid. Nothing but whispers and cold trails. We're trying to piece together a puzzle when half the pieces are missing.

Tony's club trashed, and him getting beat was another message, one we heard loud and clear. He's close, proving he doesn't give a damn who he burns to get what he's after. But unfortunately for Velasco, it didn't have the desired effect. It only threw gasoline on the fire.

The low rumble of tires crunching gravel outside draws everyone's attention. More than the fact that it's late, not many people roll up unannounced. Not unless they've got a damn good reason.

Catcher steps inside, his voice calm but alert. "Tony's here."

Riggs narrows his eyes. "Show him in." He lifts his gaze to the women. One look is all it takes. The women don't say a word and clear the room.

A beat passes, then the front door opens, and Tony walks in, favoring his left side, eyes bruised and swollen. But he carries his injuries with a kind of grit you can't fake.

Tony meets Riggs and stares from across the room. "Appreciate you seeing me." His voice is rough but steady.

Riggs nods to an empty chair. "Have a seat."

Fender pours the old man a shot of whiskey and slides it across the table. Tony accepts the drink, sipping it slowly.

Tony sets the glass down, and his eyes sweep the table as he eases onto the chair. "Not here to bitch about what happened. I'm here to give you what I got."

I lean back, crossing my arms, waiting for the old man's words.

"I know you're already digging, but I did a little of my own on this Velasco fella." Tony lets the name hang in the air like smoke. "I don't have much. No one knows what this bastard looks like. Not anyone who is still breathing, anyway. He's like a fucking ghost. People never talk to him directly. He has runners, guys who move through the shadows. Word on the street is they call him Sombra. It means shadow or some shit, depending on who you ask."

Riggs nods. "That tracks with what we know."

Tony gives a tight smile. "He doesn't just hide behind people. He becomes someone else when needed. From what I hear, he changes names, trades accents, and slips into new skin like it's nothing. You could be drinking next to him in a bar and not know it unless he wanted you to."

A chill works its way up my spine. The kind of enemy you can't see coming is the most dangerous.

Tony continues, "He's got a guy, goes by the name Tito, who acts as a middleman in Baton Rouge. I hear Tito's been active lately, recruiting muscle, paying off low-level street dealers to keep tabs on people."

"Which people?" Wick asks.

"The Kings," Tony says.

That gets everyone's attention.

"Who gave you this information?" Nova asks.

Tony's eyes flick to my brother. "Not revealing my sources. Hope you can respect that." Tony pauses. When nothing is questioned, he continues, "This source used to run with a crew that dealt on the west bank. They're small-time, but they hear things, and this Tito's been runnin' around with the club's name in his mouth. Also heard him mention the youth center, Twisted Throttle, and Kings Tactical. Seems Velasco has feelers everywhere."

Riggs leans back, arms crossed. "You said no one knows what he looks like?"

"Not even his own people. I've gathered that he's only met face-to-face with three men. One's already dead, gunshot point-blank to the temple, execution style. His body was found in a ditch outside of Lake Charles. The second, no one has seen him in over a year, and the third, well, that's Tito."

Nova scratches his jaw. "This Tito, he walks around Baton Rouge untouched?"

Tony nods. "He's got protection. You move against him, and you'll have eyes on you in minutes."

The following silence is thick, and every man at this table understands how close this threat is pressing in.

My phone buzzes in my pocket, breaking through the silence.

I pull it out.

Blocked number.

That's never a good sign, but my gut tells me to answer. "Yeah?"

"She's alive." The voice on the other end is distorted and warped, sounding like it's speaking through a tube of cardboard and static.

My pulse spikes. "Who?"

"Amara. If they haven't sold her yet."

"Where?"

"Port Allen. Abandoned warehouse. There's a shipping container. The south side of the property near the river. Number 29XB."

"Be more specific," I bark.

"Look for the old, abandoned sugar refinery. The container is in the clearing behind it."

I glance around. Everyone is watching me because they feel the shift in the air. "Who is this?" I demand, but the line goes dead. Slowly, I lower the phone, feeling the weight of every man's eye on me. "That was a tip. That woman London was lookin' for, Amara, is alive. They got her in a shipping container in Port Allen at the old sugar mill."

"I know the place," Nova says.

Tony is on his feet. "She was mine to look after. Let me help."

Riggs puts a hand up. "You're not going anywhere."

"Like hell, I ain't," Tony barks.

"No." Riggs' voice is pure steel. "You can barely move. You're more help to the club here, watchin' over the women and children with Catcher."

Tony's jaw clenches, but he reluctantly nods.

Riggs looks at Catcher. "Need the keys to your truck, brother," he says, and Catcher pulls them from his pocket, tossing them Riggs' way. "No one in or out. Got it?"

"Got it," Catcher says.

Riggs directs his attention to the rest of us, everyone checking their weapons and getting ready to roll out. "We're takin' cages and leavin' the bikes. Can't risk the noise. Some of you are with me. The others in the van," he barks, and we move fast.

The road out of New Orleans is dark, except for our headlights cutting through the long stretch of Louisiana blacktop. I'm behind the wheel of Catcher's truck, with Riggs riding shotgun. Behind us, Wick follows in the van with Nova, Kiwi, and Fender.

The hum of the tires and the occasional creak of the truck's old suspension are the only sounds filling the silence. But my head is not quiet.

Amara isn't a part of this war. She's just a young woman trying to survive who got caught up with the wrong person. She's not ours, but that doesn't matter.

We aren't saints. There's plenty of blood on our hands and bodies that will never be found. But there's a line. We won't let scum prey on the weak and look the other way. We don't sit back while a woman's life is on the line. Sometimes, we protect more than our own. Sometimes, that includes the ones with no one looking out for them.

The port smells like rust and rot, like time has forgotten the place for decades. We roll up quietly, just short of the yard's edge where the river meets the bank. There's no activity. There's no sound. The abandoned sugar mill looms in the distance, half-collapsed with jagged beams jutting toward the sky like broken ribs. Its brick walls are crumbling, and the smokestack is no longer standing.

We leave the vehicles and trek the rest of the way on foot, our boots crunching over loose gravel and overgrown weeds. We keep our eyes sharp and don't speak. Containers are scattered about the property, some stacked three high, and graffiti covers the sides of the steel boxes. Right where the anonymous caller said it would be, a solo container sits near the river's south end.

Riggs holds up a hand, and we stop, hidden behind a rusted-out forklift.

There are three guards. One is pacing slowly along the fence line near the river. Another is camped out near the back end of a semi-trailer. The third is leaning against an SUV about thirty feet from the container. A cigarette glows in the dark, lighting his face with each drag.

There are no words spoken.

Riggs gives silent commands. Each directive is precise. We fan out, circling the perimeter. The guards have no clue we're even here.

I watch Fender slip behind one of the men, a knife in his hand. One quick move, he covers the guard's mouth, dragging the blade across his throat.

Wick and I head for the smoker. He's distracted, eyes on his phone. While the dumbass is still looking down, Wick slides in behind him, grabs his head, and twists, snapping his neck like a twig. The second guard drops like a sack of bricks. The third motherfucker shouts, but Kiwi is on him, and a gunshot cracks through the air, then the third guard drops.

We rush toward the container as Kiwi digs the keys out of the dead man's pocket, tossing them to Riggs, who unlocks the padlock and pulls the double doors open.

The smell hits us first—sweat, piss, vomit, and blood.

I use the flashlight on my phone, shining it into the container.

There she is, slumped over near the back of the steel box. I head inside. The closer I get, the more I see of her. "Shit," I mutter. Her eyes are swollen shut, her lips cracked, and blood dried around her nose and mouth. She is half-naked, her shirt torn from her body, and only wearing panties. She also has deep purple bruises and welts on her thighs. I remove my cut and take off my shirt. Kneeling, I slip it over her head, putting each arm carefully through the sleeves. That's when I notice the needle marks down both arms. Anger swells inside me, knowing what she probably endured. "They've kept her doped," I say. I look at her. "Amara." I try getting a response, but get nothing. I check her pulse—it's weak, but there. Her skin is clammy, and her breathing is shallow.

She moans when I shift her, but it's a broken, ragged sound, like she's in pain but has no strength left to scream.

Riggs crouches next to me. "She needs a hospital." He stands, turning to Wick. "Dig the SUV keys off the guy you silenced." He then faces Kiwi. "Ride with them. The rest of you are with me to clean this shit up. We leave no evidence we were here."

Wick finds the key fob in the dead guy's pocket. "Load her while I start it up."

Amara is limp in my arms as I seat her in the back. Kiwi slides into the passenger seat without a word. Wick slams the driver's side door shut and hits the gas, kicking up gravel as we pull away from the yard.

"The fastest route to the nearest hospital is exit twenty-two. There's a trauma center just off the ramp."

Wick doesn't respond. He drives hard and fast.

When we hit the off-ramp, we blow through the yellow light and pull up to the emergency room entrance. Wick slams the vehicle to a stop, and I push open the door, shuffling Amara into my arms and heading for the sliding glass entrance.

Inside, the emergency room is quiet. The calm lasts two seconds. "We need some fucking help here," I boom, my voice echoing off the tiled walls like a shotgun blast.

The nurse behind the protective partition jumps to her feet and disappears. Kiwi barrels in behind me as two nurses rush out from the double doors leading to the back. I don't wait. I carry Amara down the corridor, meeting the gurney halfway where I lay her down. "She's been drugged. I don't know what." I don't rattle off more because she's wearing the evidence all over her body. I stand there for a beat as they wheel her away, hoping we arrived in time.

"Let's go before we attract unwanted attention," Kiwi says.

We don't make it out of the doors before running into trouble. Two officers walk up to us, chests puffed, hands hovering over their weapons. The lead one, a tall, square-jawed asshole with a buzzcut, runs his stern gaze over us with suspicion. The uniform following close behind him is young and looks a bit twitchy. The lead cop strides over like he's been waiting to flex on someone all day. "Who brought the girl?" His voice is raised way too loud.

I don't flinch and meet his stare. "You're lookin' at him."

The cop narrows his eyes. "Name?"

"Not givin' it," I reply.

The shorter cop steps closer into my space, thinking he can intimidate me. "Got any relation to the victim?"

"Found her." My answer is short, tone clipped.

"That's not an answer," he snaps, trying to rattle me.

"Not givin' you one," I fire back.

His partner shifts his weight from one foot to the other, his hand hovering nervously over his belt.

"I could haul your asses in right now," he says. "For interfering with an investigation, withholding information."

I stare at him, unfazed by his threat.

He opens his mouth to say something but is cut off by a third cop walking up behind him. The cop is older, with a beard, steel gray hair cropped short, and calm eyes. "Officer Bennett and Doucet," he says, his tone clipped.

Both uniforms glance his way.

"Landry," Doucet mutters.

"Go check on the victim's status. I'll take it from here," Landry orders.

Bennett scowls but doesn't argue, and Doucet looks relieved. They disappear into the hospital.

Landry shifts his attention back to Kiwi and me. It takes me a second before it clicks why I know his face. "We've met. You used to shoot at Kings Tactical."

"Everest, right?" Landry offers a handshake, and I accept. "And you're Kiwi." He looks at my brother, and he nods. Landry sighs.

"Look. I don't know what happened tonight, and I'm not asking. But a half-dead girl is gonna stir up shit. If she starts talking, the higher-ups are gonna want answers."

"You know where to find us. We got nothin' to hide," I clip.

Landry nods. "Get out of here."

As we go to leave, the sliding doors open, and a young nurse jogs out. "Wait. You two brought that poor girl in. Do you know her name?"

"Amara," I tell her.

"Last name? Does she have a family?" the nurse asks.

"Sorry, sweetheart. I don't have those answers." I go to walk away again, but stop and turn back around. "How is she?"

"Stable," she tells us, glancing between me, Kiwi, and Landry.

I give her a tight nod. "Thanks." Then we walk to where Wick is waiting with the SUV engine running.

Some time later, back at the abandoned sugar mill, the air feels thicker than before. The others are waiting when we roll up. Riggs is standing near the riverbank, his arms crossed over his chest. Next to him, Nova is crouched, washing his hands in the water while Fender lingers nearby, a cigarette dangling from his lips. Wick, Kiwi, and I approach them, my eyes scanning where the dead men once were.

"Bodies?" Wick inquires.

Riggs jerks his thumb toward the water. "Gator food."

I gaze out at the river, the water looking blacker than oil, knowing somewhere beneath the surface, three bodies are now just bones waiting to be picked clean. Then I look back at the SUV we used to transport Amara, our prints are all over it, and the last thing we need is someone thinking the Kings are linked to anything the dead men were involved with. I scan the ground, looking for something useful, and spot a length of rusty pipe near the shipping container, so I pick it up and head toward the driver's door. "Might want to move," I call out, and my brothers shift from where they stand. I wedge the pipe between the gas pedal and the seat, shift it into drive, and step back as the engine revs. The SUV lurches forward, right toward the river. It hits the bank with a hard splash, taking a few minutes before the current's pull starts taking hold, and the nose dips below the surface. It happens fast. The ass end of the SUV bobs a few times, then it's gone, swallowed by the Mississippi.

We trek back to our cages in silence. The drive back to the clubhouse is the same—a quiet that allows your thoughts to slip in and take hold. I think about our troubles, but my mind mainly focuses on returning to my woman.

We roll through the clubhouse door just past midnight, with the smell of coffee and the buzz of tension in the air.

"She alive?" Tony asks, his voice rough. He's slow to get off the sofa.

I nod once. "Yeah, but barely."

Tony lets out a slow breath of relief and closes his eyes.

Then, I spot London. She is barefoot, wearing sweatpants and one of my shirts hanging to her knees. She appears exhausted— no doubt waiting and running through every worst-case scenario in her head.

"You found her?" she asks, heading down the stairs. London crosses the room in seconds and wraps her arms around my waist, clutching at my back like she's grounding herself.

"She's in bad shape, babe. But alive." I hold her tight and bury my face in her hair.

"Listen up." Riggs grabs our attention. "It's late. Lock it down. Nobody in or out until tomorrow." Then he glances at Tony. "Tony, we'll fix you a room to crash in."

"Appreciate it, but I'm gonna head out," Tony says.

"My men aren't leavin'. That means you're stayin'. For your safety." Riggs' tone is firm.

Tony looks like he wants to argue, but he doesn't.

Because that's the end of it.

London takes my hand, and I follow her without a word to our room. The dim light from the bedside lamp glows softly against the walls, and the sheets are a mess, like she tried to sleep but couldn't.

I pause in the center of the room, wound tight, and my mind won't shut off. And somewhere deep in my chest, something tight is unraveling.

London steps in front of me, pushes my cut off my shoulders, and hangs it on the footboard. She doesn't ask what happened to my shirt. Actually, she doesn't speak at all. She undoes my belt buckle, slowly removes it, and drops it to the floor. Then she leads me to the bed, and I sit on the edge where she kneels and removes my boots one by one.

I let her do it.

Because it's what I didn't know I needed.

Just her.

Just the silence.

We crawl into bed, and I pull her close, burying my face in the curve of her neck, breathing my woman in. London wraps her arms around me, holding me like I am hers.

There are no expectations.

Only her heartbeat against mine.

For now, the unrest and tension my body holds, caused by the threat looming above us, dissipates.

16

LONDON

When I wake, Kallum's heat is at my back, his hand pressed against my pussy while his finger teases my clit and his bare cock rubs against my backside. His teeth gently nip at my neck, making my breath hitch. His lips smile against my sensitive flesh when he realizes I'm awake. I arch my back and grind my ass against his cock. Instead of giving me what I crave, he continues to tease me by rubbing circles over my clit. It's not enough. I want him inside me. "Kallum, please."

"What do you want, baby?" he asks.

"I want you to stop playing and fuck me already."

Does he listen? Nope.

He's gotten me so wet that the inside of my thighs is soaked. Having had enough, I reach back and grab a fistful of his hair while looking him square in the eyes. "Goddamn it, Kallum."

Kallum smiles that annoying smirk reserved only for me. The one where I've given him exactly what he wants and, in a flash, both of our bodies roll until Kallum is flat on his back, and I'm sitting upward while straddling his hips.

Still dazed, I peer back over my shoulder and study Kallum's face as I begin grinding my wet pussy against the base of his cock. "Two can play at this game," I rasp.

A muscle in Kallum's jaw twitches, and he bucks beneath me, then digs his fingers into my hips. "That's not how this works."

In an instant, he lifts effortlessly and then slams me back down onto his cock. We both groan as he fills me completely. I grind my hips, taking him deeper. Kallum's fingers curl around my hips to the point of pain, but I love it.

"Fuck, your pussy is choking the hell out of my dick," he growls.

His words only encourage me to move, so I raise my hips and then slowly slide back down. Closing my eyes, I repeat the move over and over until the sound of our wet bodies slapping together fills the room. I yelp when Kallum's palm smacks against my ass cheek. "Open your eyes and watch," he orders.

Doing as I'm told, I open my eyes and stare straight ahead. A gasp escapes my mouth when I see myself in the reflection of the dresser mirror in front of the bed. I almost don't recognize the woman staring back at me. My hair is wild, my eyes are glazed over with lust, and my face is flushed. Suddenly, my gaze connects with Kallum's in the mirror.

"Look how beautiful you are ridin' my cock."

He's right.

I look good.

We look good.

Kallum and I fit together perfectly.

Dragging my nails along his thighs, I keep a steady pace, all while watching our reflection.

"Tell me you're close," Kallum grits out.

"I'm close," I confess. Tears prick at the corners of my eyes as my release builds and my pussy starts to pulse around his cock.

"Fuck, I can feel you comin'." Kallum thrust his hips upward.

That's all it takes. On a cry, my orgasm slams through me.

Behind me, Kallum curses through heaving breaths as he follows me over the edge.

Later that morning, Promise and I arrive at the office the same way we have the past couple of days, with Catcher as our shadow. Zara is there waiting for us when we walk in. Since she has to drop her son off at preschool early every morning, she comes straight to the office to prepare Promise's and my calendars and to make coffee. And if we have client meetings in the office that day, she ensures beverages and snacks are prepared and in the conference room.

"Morning, guys," Zara greets us with a smile.

"Morning, Zara."

Zara stands and walks around her desk. "London, Mrs. Wells had to reschedule her eight-thirty appointment for this Friday. However, I took a call from a gentleman about ten minutes ago who insisted on meeting with you." Zara looks down at her tablet. "Mr. Harrison. He said you were recommended by a friend of his. He sounded rather desperate, so I put him down for eight-thirty since Mrs. Wells rescheduled. I hope that's okay. If not, I can call him back."

I wave my hand. "No, no. That's fine. I'll take the meeting. Thanks, Zara."

Zara looks down at her watch. "Mr. Harrison should be here in fifteen minutes. I'll set the conference room up."

Catcher takes his post in the corner of the waiting room while Promise disappears down the hall toward her office. "I have some calls to make," she calls out over her shoulder. "Let me know if you need anything."

On my way to my office, Zara passes me holding a cup of coffee, a paper plate filled with a couple of donuts, and a ham and cheese bagel. She heads straight for the waiting area where

Catcher is sitting and passes him the food and coffee. I smile at how well Zara has gotten used to his presence.

Once in my office, I store my purse in the cabinet beside my desk and grab a notepad, pen, and laptop before heading into the conference room. Just as I settle into one of the chairs, Zara appears at the door. "Hey, Mr. Harrison just arrived. You still have a few minutes. Do you want me to have him take a seat out there or send him back?"

"I'm ready for him. You can send him back."

Zara nods and dips out of the room. A few seconds later, she returns with a man close behind.

Standing, I make my way around the table to greet him. "You must be Mr. Harrison." I offer the man my hand and a warm smile. "I'm Ms. Monroe."

I take in the man standing before me. He's at least six feet tall and slim but has broad shoulders. His hair is dark brown, almost black, and he has brown eyes. I'd put him at around mid to late thirties. I can't note anything remarkable about the man, but he exudes confidence and has an air of authority. He's dressed in a sharp suit, perfectly tailored to his build and height. I don't miss the Rolex on his wrist when he takes my hand. Also, I don't miss the gold cufflinks he's sporting. The man obviously comes from money or is successful in his own right, which has me wondering why he's looking to hire me. Not that I'm not a damn good attorney, but guys like Mr. Harrison tend to lean toward the more popular firms downtown that cater to the elite and wealthy. Birds of a feather and all that jazz.

"Nice to meet you, Ms. Monroe. Thank you for agreeing to meet with me on such short notice." Mr. Harrison smiles. I'll admit Mr. Harrison has a great smile with perfectly straight white teeth, but he lacks those little lines at the corners of his eyes, which tell me he doesn't smile too often.

"It's no problem at all, Mr. Harrison." I gesture toward the chair at the end of the table. "Please, have a seat."

Mr. Harrison inclines his head and takes a seat.

"Before we get started, would you like anything to drink? We have coffee, juice, or bottled water."

"How kind of you, Ms. Monroe, but I'm good."

I nod and sit across from him. "Why don't we start with why you are here today?" I open my laptop and prepare to take notes. When Mr. Harrison doesn't say anything, I look up from my computer to find him watching me, his gaze assessing. I'm not sure what to make of the man just yet, as he seems relaxed with his impeccable posture. One hand rests on top of the table while the other is casually draped over the arm of the chair. Yet, there is something about Mr. Harrison that raises questions, and I just can't put my finger on why.

Finally, he speaks, "I want to divorce my wife."

"Okay." I keep my tone even and wait for Mr. Harrison to elaborate.

"Six months ago, I started to suspect she was having an affair, so I hired a private detective. It didn't take him long to confirm my suspicions."

My face softens. "I'm sorry to hear that, Mr. Harrison."

Mr. Harrison continues, "I don't wish to go after her for alimony. I seek a clean break. The only problem is I know she will likely fight the divorce and, at the very least, try to get her hands on as much of my money as possible."

I stop typing and look up from my computer. "So, no splitting of the assets? You want to leave her with nothing?" I ask, keeping my tone neutral.

"She can leave with what she came into the marriage with… nothing," Mr. Harrison states without a shred of emotion.

"So, you feel your wife will contest the divorce?"

"Yes."

"How long have you and your wife been married?" I ask.

"Twelve years."

"Any children?"

Mr. Harrison shakes his head. "No children."

I nod and put that in my notes. "Do you have any joint accounts or property with your wife?"

"No. She doesn't work, and everything is in my name."

"What are your thoughts on spousal support?"

"Absolutely not. My wife doesn't get a dime."

It's not uncommon for people to disassociate from their emotions as they go through a divorce, especially after finding out a spouse has cheated, but there is something—I don't know—*off* about Mr. Harrison. I've heard stories like his more times than I can count. They are a dime a dozen. But the man in front of me is talking about his marriage and his wife cheating like he's reading from a script.

"You mentioned something about a private investigator before. I'm assuming you can provide proof of your wife's affair."

Before he replies, Mr. Harrison studies me for a long time, almost to the point of making me uncomfortable. "That is correct."

Ignoring his odd behavior, I push forward. "If you wish to proceed with my services, I'll need to see the evidence in question."

"I'll bring everything you need soon, Ms. Monroe. I look forward to handling this unfortunate matter as soon as possible. For all involved."

Something about the way Mr. Harrison says that last part doesn't bode well with me.

Thankfully, Zara chooses that moment to interrupt. "I'm sorry to interrupt, but you have a call on line two. They say it's urgent."

"Thank you, Zara." I stand. "I'm so sorry, Mr. Harrison. I'll have to take this."

Mr. Harrison follows suit by pushing his chair back. "Not a problem, Ms. Monroe. I must be going anyway."

"If you wouldn't mind leaving your contact information with my assistant, I'll be in touch soon to discuss how you'd like to proceed and what I'll need from you."

"Of course. I'll be sure to do that." Mr. Harrison places his hand on the small of my back as I lead him out of the conference room. His touch sends shivers down my spine, and not the good kind.

He reaches into his pocket and hands me a business card printed with his name and number. Without another word, he strolls down the hall, hands firmly placed in his suit pants. He doesn't spare Zara a glance before he exits the building.

"Hey. You okay?" Promise steps out into the hallway.

Shaking my head, I decide all the drama that's been wreaking havoc on my life lately has me on edge and overthinking everything. "Yeah, I'm good."

Then I remember the phone call waiting for me. "Shoot." I snap my fingers. "I have a call waiting." I rush into my office and snatch the receiver from the landline on my desk, but when I put the phone to my ear, all I get is dial tone.

***

By seven in the evening, I'm bone tired and ready to get back to the clubhouse. All I want is a glass of wine and a hot shower. Promise left a couple of hours ago when Nova came to pick her up, and Zara left shortly after. I stayed behind to meet with Missy Tyler, a single mother who is currently in a nasty custody battle with her ex-husband. Missy works full-time and has an asshole boss who won't allow her time off work, so on the days I meet with her, I extend my own hours to accommodate her schedule. Raised by a single mother, I know firsthand how difficult it is to juggle work and life.

"Ready?" Catcher sticks his head in my office.

"Yep. Just let me grab my purse." I open the bottom drawer of my desk and retrieve my things. "Mind if we stop by Jonny's on the way? I want to pick up a bottle of wine."

Catcher pulls out his phone. "Yeah. I'll give Everest a heads up." And we head out.

The drive to Jonny's Liquor is out of the way, but he always has my favorite wine in stock, so it's worth the drive. On the way, Catcher follows close behind on his bike. When we pull into the parking lot, Catcher parks beside my driver's side door. As I climb out, I watch him scan our surroundings. Not only is Jonny's in the opposite direction of the clubhouse, but it's in a bad part of town —I'm talking bars on the windows, bad part of town—however, like I said, he carries the good stuff. Also, I like Jonny. He's a good guy. Jonny was due to retire last year, but his wife of thirty-two years was diagnosed with breast cancer. Their social security and retirement alone wouldn't cover her treatments, so he stays open in order to care for her. I suppose I could shop at another store and simply request they carry my favorite wine, but my loyalty lies with Jonny.

As we walk up to the store, I notice Catcher's attention is elsewhere, and I follow his gaze to the empty parking lot across the street. A silver four-door sedan with tinted windows is parked in front of a closed dry cleaner. I can't see who is in the car, but I know someone is there by the cigarette smoke billowing through the cracked driver's side window. "Everything okay?" I ask.

Catcher jerks his chin, motioning me to keep moving, but he doesn't say anything. I shrug my shoulders and take that as a sign not to worry. A bell chimes when we walk through the store door, alerting Jonny to our arrival. I spot him sitting on a stool behind the cash register. A television with the local news playing is mounted on a wall above his head.

A huge grin stretches across his weathered face when he sees me. "London! How come you haven't been by to see me? How have you been?"

"Hey, Mr. Jonny. Work has been keeping me busy. How's Sherlene?"

"Sherlene is hangin' in there." Mr. Jonny's face lights up at the mention of his wife. "She just started takin' a water aerobics class down at the Y. My Sherlene is keepin' those kids down there on their toes."

I laugh. "I have no doubt about that. I'm glad to hear she's doing well." I move to the back of the store, where the wine is stocked. "You got the good stuff!" I call out.

"You know it. Top shelf, darlin'."

I spot what I'm looking for and snag two bottles off the shelf. When I return to the front, Catcher still hovers by the door. Only now, his face is hard, and he's holding his gun.

"Catcher, what's going on?" I can't help the tremble in my voice.

"We need to go *now*," he clips.

I nod and, with shaky hands, reach into my purse and pull out some cash. "Here, Mr. Jonny. Keep the change." I set the money down on the counter.

Mr. Jonny looks from me to Catcher. "You all right, dear?"

I swallow. "I'll be okay."

Mr. Jonny has lived in New Orleans his whole life. He knows who Catcher is and who the Kings are, so he knows I'm in no danger with Catcher. But when I see him pull his shotgun out from under the counter, I realize he also senses danger. Jonny is no stranger to being robbed. However, whatever has Catcher on high alert has nothing to do with a robbery. When I peek over Catcher's shoulder, I glimpse that car we saw parked across the street when we first arrived, only now it's rolling into the liquor store parking lot.

"Do you know who that is?" I ask Catcher.

He shakes his head. "No. But I don't like his looks." Catcher pulls out his phone.

Mr. Jonny walks out from behind the counter, shotgun in hand. "Want me to call the police?"

As soon as the words spill from Mr. Jonny's mouth, a hail of gunfire rips through the storefront window. Shards of broken glass fly all around me, and I scream. The wind is knocked out of my lungs when Catcher's large body slams into me. On the debris-riddled floor, he uses his body to shield mine while whoever is outside continues to shoot. Bullets rip through Jonny's store for what feels like forever until suddenly the shooting stops and is replaced by deathly silence. The only thing I can hear is the rapid beating of my heart and Catcher's heavy breathing.

"Oh my God. What the fuck?" I start to panic, and then I remember Mr. Jonny. "Mr. Jonny!" I call out as I try to push Catcher off me.

"He's good," Catcher rumbles, shifting slightly.

I look to my left and see Mr. Jonny crouched down behind a display shelf. He has a cut on his forearm that's bleeding, but otherwise appears unharmed. I breathe a sigh of relief.

"Stay low," Catcher orders. Gun in hand, he slowly and cautiously creeps over to the window, stretches his neck, and peeks out. "Fuck." He drops back down.

"What did you see?" I whisper.

"Four men," he tells me. "One in the car, driver's side, two standing out front, and one approaching the building on the right."

"Here." Mr. Jonny digs in his front pocket, pulls out a set of keys, and slides them across the floor toward Catcher. "My truck is parked out back. I'll hold them sons of bitches off while you get London out of here."

"What?" I shake my head. "No. You have to come with us. We are not leaving you here." I look at Catcher. "We are *not* leaving him here."

I watch Mr. Jonny and Catcher share a look.

"Go." Mr. Jonny jerks his chin and then goes to where Catcher is posted.

Catcher grits his teeth and then moves.

I go to argue when he grabs hold of my arm. "Catcher," I hiss.

"Go with Catcher, sweetheart," Mr. Jonny urges. "I can take care of myself."

"Let's move." Catcher doesn't give me time to say anything else before he's practically dragging me across the floor. "Keep low and stay behind me."

I take one last look at Jonny over my shoulder as I follow Catcher to the back of the store toward the emergency exit. He gives me a reassuring nod. In front of me, Catcher pauses. He and Mr. Jonny share one last look. Mr. Jonny nods and cocks his gun. Moments later, the air fills with the sound of gunfire once again.

When Catcher and I reach the rear exit, he pushes the door open a smidge and peeks out. Sensing we are clear, he reminds me, "Stay close," then we make a run for it. Parked about thirty feet from us is a pick-up truck. Just as we reach the driver's side door, a bullet pierces the window, followed by another blast. Catcher's body jerks and slams into the side of the truck. Without hesitation, he returns fire, killing the guy. I scream and cover my head when a bullet whizzes past. That's when I notice two more guys rounding the corner of the building.

"Get in the fuckin' truck, *now*!" Catcher bellows.

I shove open the door and dive into the truck. As Catcher tosses me the keys, I notice blood soaking through his shirt over his shoulder. "Oh my God, Catcher. You've been shot."

Catcher continues to return fire, and the two men duck behind the dumpster. Just as he goes to climb into the truck behind me, three more shots ring out. Catcher grunts as his body slumps against the truck's driver's seat before slumping to the ground. I watch in horror as blood pours from a hole in his chest.

For as long as I live, I will never forget the gurgling sound currently coming from his mouth.

"Catcher." I choke on a sob.

Go, he mouths, his eyes wide and trained on my face.

Tears stream down my face at the thought of leaving him behind, but I have to get help. So, as much as it pains me, I slam the truck door and shove the keys into the ignition. Eyes blurry with tears, I put the truck in gear and step on the gas. The truck's back tires kick up dust and gravel as I peel out of the parking lot. I look in the rear-view mirror and catch sight of a car pulling up beside where Catcher's body lies unmoving on the ground, as two men jump into the back seat and give chase. I swipe away my tears with the back of my hand and focus on the road in front of me. But just as I'm about to turn left out of the parking lot, a white van cuts me off, forcing me to slam on my brakes. The van stops in front of me while the car boxes me in from behind. The two men in the car jump out. One approaches the passenger side while the other approaches the driver's side. I engage the locks, hoping to keep them out.

"Fuck, London, *think.*"

The man at my door bangs on the window. "Give it up, bitch," he sneers.

Refusing to it give up, I put the truck in reverse and slam my foot on the pedal, ramming into the car behind me. I repeat this maneuver again when I shift into drive and ram the van blocking me. The asshole standing in front of the truck is forced to jump out of the way to avoid being crushed. Too bad I missed.

"You crazy fucking bitch," he spits.

Just as I'm about to shift the truck into reverse, the guy I almost hit puts his fist through my window, shattering it. I climb over the center console, but I'm not quick enough. The door is wrenched open, and a hand clamps down around my ankle, pulling me back. Twisting to my back, I bend my other knee, and with all the force I can muster, I kick the motherfucker square in the nose, and he roars with pain as blood seeps from his nose. When he loses his grip on my ankle, I crawl over to the passenger seat, open the door, and jump out of the truck. The second that both feet hit the pavement, I take off. I don't get ten feet before I'm tackled from behind, and the guy on top of me knocks the air from my lungs and shoves my face into the gravel.

"Tase the cunt, Rico," I hear another guy say.

The next thing I know, it's lights out.

"Hey," someone whispers. "Hey, are you okay?" the voice says again. I blink my eyes open and, through blurred vision, try to locate the source.

"She's waking up." Beside me, I hear shuffling. I try to move, but my body feels stiff. "Where am I?" I ask, confused. My vision clears, and a young woman no older than nineteen or twenty appears.

"We don't know where we're at. None of us saw where we were brought. We just woke up in this room together."

I sit up and lean against the wall, ignoring how badly my body aches. Then, I get a good look at my surroundings. My heart drops when I realize what the girls mean by 'us.' There are seven other women in here besides me, and none of us knows where here is. "How long have you all been here?"

"I've been here two days. My name is Anna."

"I'm London."

Anna points to a blonde-haired girl. "That's Sara. Then you have Olivia, Karmen, Brianna, Dee, and Marcy. Olivia and Dee have been here the longest. Five days."

"And none of you know where we are?" I ask.

"No," Marcy answers. "The guys who brought us here don't talk to us. They just come by once a day to bring us food."

I look around the small room. It's barren aside from a single lamp. There is no furniture, and the carpet looks old and dingy. It smells like sweat and mildew. Off to the side of the room is a bathroom. Standing, I walk over to the door and find it locked. Beside the door is a boarded-up window. Everyone startles when the sound of the lock on the door engages. I take two steps back when the door swings open. Standing in front of me is the bastard I kicked in the face. I smirk when I get a good look at his slightly crooked and swollen nose. The guy conveys his displeasure by stepping forward and backhanding me across the face. I counteract by lunging at him. And because he's taken off guard by my actions, I'm able to get several kicks in, including another blow to his nose, making it gush blood once again.

"Enough," a new voice barks at the same time I'm being pulled off the son of bitch. Once I'm contained, I get a good look at the other guy, who is now picking his bleeding friend up off the floor. "You're a fucking disgrace, Carlos. Boss is going to be pissed you marked one of the girls."

"The fucking bitch broke my goddamn nose, man."

"We don't have time for you to be a pussy, Carlos. Boss is waiting for us at the port. He wants us to bring the girls." The asshole sweeps his gaze across the room to where the girls are huddled. "Tie them up and bag them." Then he pins me with a stare. The asshole tries to intimidate me, but I'm not deterred. I match his energy with an equal look of disgust.

17

EVEREST

The clubhouse is quiet. It's almost too calm for my liking, and not sitting right. The hairs on the back of my neck have been standing up since London texted that she was staying late at the office to finish up with one more client, then swinging by Jonny's for a bottle of wine. I shouldn't feel on edge knowing Catcher is with her, but I can't shake this unease settling in my chest.

Her GPS ping has been locked in place in front of Jonny's liquor for thirty minutes.

I recheck the app on my phone, tapping the screen with my thumb and refreshing it, hoping it will show her in motion. It doesn't.

"You've checked that phone more times than Kiwi looks at himself in the mirror, " Nova says, lounging on one of the worn leather sofas with Promise tucked into his side.

I look at him but don't respond, then recheck my phone.

"She still at Jonny's?" Promise asks. "She texted me when she got there, asking if us women wanted red or white tonight."

"Too long for my likin'," I mutter, staring at my phone screen, waiting for the dot to move.

"Jonny probably got her and Catcher stalled. You know how the old man likes to talk," Riggs states.

Maybe.

But one thing about my woman is that she doesn't linger when she's had a long day and wants wine.

The weight of Velasco's threat hangs heavy. It's been weeks of knowing we're on the motherfucker's radar, with minimal leads to his whereabouts or even what the bastard looks like. It's like trying to catch a damn fart. You can smell the stench it leaves, but can't see it.

My phone rings, with Jonny's number lighting up the screen, then my stomach clenches as I answer. "Jonny?" The instant I say his name, the buzz in the room fades, and every eye falls on me.

"Everest," his voice is frantic, winded, and pained. "God help me... they took her."

I stop breathing.

"What?"

"They hit the store with guns drawn. They shot up the place." He pauses, trying to catch his breath. "Catcher is down. He put himself between them and London. He took bullets to the chest and gut. It's bad, really bad."

"Fuck." I'm on my feet, pulling at my hair, with nowhere to direct the wave of emotions slamming into my chest.

My world narrows to a single blinding point.

Blood pounds in my ears.

"Jonny. Listen to me. Do not let the cops touch the security feed." It's taking every ounce of restraint I have so as not to lose control.

"You got it," he swears.

"Good. We're on our way." I hang up.

The moment I lower the phone, the silence in the clubhouse is suffocating.

"Talk." Riggs is already on his feet.

"Men shot up Jonny's. They took London." The words feel like broken glass in my throat. "Catcher is down. Jonny says it's bad." I swallow hard.

Suddenly, everyone springs into action, rapidly checks their weapons, and approaches the door, each step fueled by urgency as Riggs barks orders. "Nova, Kiwi. Stay here. Lock this place down tight. If there's any activity outside this clubhouse, shoot first."

The air is thick and charged with the pressure you feel in your chest before lightning strikes as we burst through the clubhouse door. No one speaks. We're all locked in and focused. Me? I'm riding a razor-thin edge between fury and control while my pulse jackhammers in my throat.

I throw my leg over my bike, start the engine, and twist the throttle, kicking up gravel and dust as I pull away. Leaving the clubhouse in my wake, my brothers behind me, our tires scream against the asphalt.

By the time we roll up to Jonny's, the scene is a damn war zone of flashing red and blue lights. We park our bikes where we can and push through the building crowd just as Catcher is being hauled out on a stretcher, with an EMT actively performing CPR. My boots hit the pavement hard as I rush toward him. His cut is soaked through, red blooming across his chest and abdomen. There's so much of it. His skin is pale and he looks like death.

The first responders waste no time loading our brother into the back of the ambulance and taking off.

My stomach sinks as I stand with Riggs, Wick, and Fender, our eyes fixed on the ambulance's taillights.

"He's a fighter. He'll pull through," Riggs says, but uncertainty lingers in his tone. There's something unsettling in the air, an unspoken fear that clings to us all like a heavy fog as the ambulance disappears.

My gaze drifts and lands on Jonny sitting on the curb, hunched and clutching a blood-soaked towel to his forearm. His usually neat white hair is stained red, plastered to his forehead. His glasses are missing, and his lip is split.

The three of us push through the crowd that has gathered. I crouch in front of Jonny. He spots us. "Footage is in the back of my office. Password *Whodat*." He holds out a key. "Office door is locked," he says.

Riggs grabs the key, passing it to Fender. "Get the footage." He looks down the sidewalk, and I shift my attention to a cop he's locked in on. "Wick, you and Everest stay with Jonny. I'm gonna buy Fender time to get what we need," Riggs says and walks away.

Jonny hangs his head. "I'm so fucking sorry." He looks up at me, then stares past me with a glassy look in his eyes.

My hands curl into fists so tight my knuckles pop.

Another ambulance rolls onto the scene. I stand slowly, rage pulsing in my veins. I don't speak as the EMTs approach us. I've got nothing against Jonny. He did what he could. My anger is directed at the men who took my woman and are the reason my brother is fighting for his life.

"You hear these motherfuckers say anything. A name?"

Jonny squeezes his eyes shut, attempting to remember any detail that will help give us direction. "I'm sorry, no." Jonny is loaded onto a stretcher, but before they roll him away, he grabs my arm. "Make them pay," he says, his voice taking on a darker tone.

Wasting no more time, Wick and I slip past the yellow tape and enter the liquor store. Inside, it looks like a scene out of a movie—nothing I haven't seen before, but it hits differently. There are collapsed shelves throughout the store, bottles of liquor shattered, broken glass everywhere, and the linoleum floor is covered with a thick layer of red. Near the register, slumped in another pool of blood, is the guy Catcher took down, his mask half off his face, and a bullet right through the temple.

A few seconds later, we're crammed into Jonny's office at the rear of the store. Fender has the security footage pulled up with a multiscreen feed from the store. He's hacked into the city and parish traffic systems in another window. We watch in horror as the scene unfolds on the computer screen. My heart races, and a cold wave of dread washes over me when I see my brother being shot. As the chaos continues, my eyes fixate on my woman fighting for her life before being taken. A knot tightens in my stomach. Then, Fender focuses on time-stamped images from the traffic cams.

"There." He points. "The same van headed east. I lose them after they leave the main roads."

"Where's the last ping?" Riggs asks.

"Industrial zone. There are no cameras out there. Just warehouses, junkyards, and this." He clicks a thumbnail, pulling up a satellite image of a dilapidated, abandoned hotel busted and surrounded by cracked asphalt and overgrowth.

"That's the old Admiral Inn. It's been vacant for years, used by squatters, drug deals, and it's a known sex trafficking drop point."

My pulse spikes.

"Then that's where we look first," Riggs says.

We head to our bikes, and a short time later, we roll up on the old, ground-level hotel. The place looks like a graveyard, long abandoned, half swallowed by weeds and rot. The air out here is heavy, stagnant, and sour. Thick with something vile. Worst of all is the silence. We dismount fast, weapons drawn.

"We clear it room by room," Riggs orders, his tone leaves no room for argument.

Wick breaks off toward the back of the building. Riggs moves south. I head north, weapon drawn, heart thundering, and London on my mind.

I enter the first room, the hinges creaking, and step inside. The stench of mildew, mixed with rat feces, hits me first. My boots crunch over broken glass and used needles. The room is empty. There's nothing here but a reminder of how far people can fall. I move on to the room next door. There's a stained mattress on the floor, restraints hanging from an eye hook on the wall above it.

That sight alone nearly drops me to my knees.

The other rooms I clear tell the same story—an empty space and no trace of my woman. My chest tightens, and dread claws its way up my throat like a monster trying to rip me open from the inside.

She was here.

I feel it.

And I am too late.

"Place is empty." I hear Wick's voice just outside the room.

I let out a roar and slam my fist through the window. Glass explodes around my hand, pain blooming in my knuckles, blood trickling down my fingers.

We have nothing.

No direction.

No fucking time.

Then, my phone buzzes in my cut pocket, and I yank it out like it might explode.

Blocked number.

The hair on the back of my neck stands up.

I answer, each word deliberate, like ice sliding off my tongue. "Who the fuck is this?"

There's a pause.

Then, laughter. It's distorted and warped like it's coming from a broken speaker—different than before. The laugh is low and sinister. This motherfucker is enjoying himself, playing with me.

My stomach drops like I stepped off a cliff.

I put him on speaker.

"Velasco?" I growl.

"Perhaps." There's a second of silence, then, "You want her..." the voice drawls, followed by another laugh, deeper this time, malicious. "Come get her."

My feet feel like they're sinking into the concrete, and my jaw clenches so tightly I taste blood.

The voice chuckles again, slower.

Then it's quiet again.

"SouthPort. By the River." Another pause. "I'll be waiting."

The line goes dead.

"The bastard is fuckin' with us," Fender seethes.

My hands curl into fists. The quiet inside me is worse than the rage. It's a hollow space where something dark hides, needing to destroy something and not stopping until it does. Whoever the fuck it is, just put a match to the gasoline I've been drowning in since London was taken.

I don't stop to think. I move. My feet carry me across the empty lot. Ready to kill every one of them.

"Hold it." Riggs barks behind me, causing me to freeze. "I already have one man lying on an operating table who might not survive. I'm not putting another one in the ground. Get your head right before we do this." The steel in his voice cuts deep, each word hitting like a blade to the gut, sharp with truth.

I nod once, keeping my mouth shut.

"He knows we're coming. When we get there, we move fast and don't stop," Riggs says, eyeing each of us. "We leave no man alive. We spill blood for our brother. This ends tonight." Then Riggs looks back at me. "Let's go get your woman."

The port is quiet in an eerie, unnatural way, as if it knows death is near. Our current location is isolated, dimmer, and cut off from the rest of the property by a long stretch of rusted fencing.

I'm vibrating, every muscle in my body wired tight, my trigger finger twitching, and my heart pounding like it's trying to break out of my chest. Steel walls rise around us, containers stacked high as we weave our way straight into the belly of the beast toward the southeast side of the yard—weapons up, no words.

She's here, somewhere in this goddamn maze.

I'm here, baby. I'm coming for you.

Suddenly, a man with a rifle steps out from the shadows. I don't hesitate and put a bullet in his chest. His body jerks backward, slamming into the side of a steel box. We keep moving as another man charges us, his weapon raised. Wick puts three rounds into his body.

"Move, move," Riggs growls, sweeping left.

We charge deeper into the yard, cutting through narrow lanes between containers. Gunfire erupts, and bullets ping off the steel surrounding us.

We crouch, taking cover.

Riggs clocks the culprit, hiding behind a forklift. He takes aim and fires one shot, and the motherfucker is dead. Fender pivots and fires twice, knocking another man clean off his feet.

We press forward, keeping our momentum.

The river is louder now, slapping against the banks. We've made it to the southeast side of the port.

A slow movement flickers at the edge of my vision, and out of the darkness emerges a shadow, a gun aimed in our direction. His steps are deliberate, each echoing with a menacing weight that heightens my pulse as the air around us thickens.

We aim at the motherfucker.

He doesn't flinch.

I move forward. "Velasco," I growl.

He smiles, slow and unsettling. He doesn't confirm or deny his identity. Instead, he takes a drag and flicks a cigarette to the dirt. "You came for the bitch but walked into your own funeral." His voice is smooth and cold.

"Where is she?" I demand, my fingers curling tighter on the trigger.

He tilts his head. "Sold goods. Some twisted fuck out of Croatia is already foaming at the mouth to get his hands on that spitfire. He likes them loud. He likes to break them."

I see red and take another step forward.

The bastard chuckles. "Maybe I'll take her for a spin myself."

"Not while I'm breathin'," I seethe, my voice lethal.

He chuckles again, deeper this time, and raises an eyebrow. "That can be arranged."

I'm done.

I don't wait for another word to move past the asshole's lips.

I shoot him in the chest.

He stumbles, his eyes wide in shock, but unfortunately, he's still breathing. Still fucking laughing. He drops to his knees, coughing, with spit trailing down his chin. "You're dead men walking." He grins, crimson foam bubbling from his lips.

I walk up, gun steady, look down at him, and pull the trigger, cutting off his twisted laugh and splitting his skull like a melon. The bastard is dead, but I find no relief. I won't until I see London.

Looking at the containers, I run and start ripping open doors, frantically searching for her.

The others jump into action.

"Back here!" Fender shouts, and I head toward the sound of his voice.

I round the corner as Wick bashes the lock off a red container near the river's edge.

The doors groan when he pulls them open.

And there she is.

London.

Huddled with a few other women.

She is hooded, her wrists bound behind her back, and blood splatters on her clothes.

"London," I say her name to help me breathe as I rush inside.

"Kallum?" she calls out in a tone of relief that damn near causes my knees to buckle out from under me.

I rip the hood off. London's lip is swollen, with a cut to her cheek and dried blood all over her. Her eyes snap to mine, and her body falls into my arms, where she belongs. "I got you, baby," I whisper, my voice raw.

She pulls back just enough to look at me. "About damn time."

I let out a heavy breath. "Never lettin' you outta my sight again."

Her brows lift. "That mean I'm moving in?"

This woman.

"It means you already did."

I let go of her long enough to get my knife and slice through the zip ties bound tight around her wrists. Then, I drag my eyes over her, looking for other injuries.

"It's not my blood, Kallum." Her voice is softer, and she turns, looking up at me. "Is he..." Her lip quivers, leaving her question hanging, but I know what she's asking.

"Last we heard, he was heading to surgery. We don't know yet, baby."

"He was protecting me."

"I know." I pull her into my chest, and she clings to me.

Riggs, Wick, and Fender help the other women by cutting restraints and leading them out of the steel container with London at my side.

Riggs walks up, his eyes on London. "You good, sweetheart?"

London nods. "I am now."

Riggs then turns to me. "Take your woman home. We got it from here."

I clasp my hand on his shoulder. "Let me know when you receive news on Catcher?"

"I'll keep you updated. Now get outta here," Riggs orders, and I don't argue.

I sweep London off her feet.

"I can walk," she protests.

I ignore her. "Just shut up and let me take care of you, woman." I start walking.

London sighs, and I'm half-ass expecting her to say something else with that sassy mouth. Instead, she wraps her arms around my neck and buries her face into my throat.

I press on, not once looking back, knowing my brothers will take care of the aftermath and get the women to safety.

Right now, I'm holding onto the only thing that matters.

And I'm never letting her go.

The following day, I lay in bed, feeling the soft warmth of London snuggled into my side. Her gentle breath creates a soothing rhythm, wrapping me in comfort. But the room feels unbearably quiet, making the silence press against me like a heavy blanket, amplifying my thoughts.

I glance at her peaceful face, the way her hair spills across the pillow, and I wish I could freeze this moment in time. Yet the stillness weighs on me, and I can't shake the feeling that something is off.

The weight of everything we just went through hasn't settled. It hangs in the air, choking out the peace we should feel. I should feel relieved, but I still feel rage simmering beneath the surface of my skin because my brother is fighting for his life.

I got the text just after sunrise.

Riggs: *Still critical. Doesn't look good.*

Nothing needs to be said out loud.

Catcher took bullets protecting my woman, and there's nothing I can do for him but hold the woman he was willing to give the ultimate sacrifice for.

London stirs beside me, her arm draped across my chest, fingers dragging down the ink over my ribs. "You're thinking too loud," she murmurs. "Is it C-Catcher?" Her voice cracks.

"Yeah, babe. He's not doin' good." I press a kiss to her temple. "I'll make coffee. Then we'll meet the others at the hospital." I climb out of bed and pull on a pair of sweats before glancing back at London, who's stretching, the sheet falling, exposing her breasts.

"I'm going to shower." She stands, wearing nothing but the sass she wore to bed. "Join me if you want me to suck the soul right out of ya." She winks.

I grin despite the lingering knot in my chest. "You make one hell of an offer, babe."

She hums, disappearing into the bathroom with that sway in her hips that should be illegal.

I step into the kitchen and fire up the coffeemaker. I'm still rolling the tension out of my shoulders when there's a knock at the door.

I'm not expecting company, but every part of me tenses. I grab my weapon, flip the safety, keeping the barrel low and out of sight, and move to the door. "Who is it?" I bark.

"Detective Broussard," the voice outside the door replies. "New Orleans PD. I'm investigating the incident at Jonny's Liquor. I need to ask a few questions."

I slide the chain into place and crack the door open just enough to get a look at the motherfucker. He's a man in his mid-forties with a thick, short beard, a button-down shirt, and a badge clipped to his belt. There's nothing off about him at first glance.

"ID," I demand.

He lifts his wallet and flips it open. *It looks legit.*

"Just a moment of your time," he says.

I close the door and put my gun away, hiding it behind a small box of motorcycle parts. I unlatch the chain and open the door. "Make it quick."

He steps in, his eyes scanning the area. "Nice place."

"Ask your questions. I'm not guaranteeing I'll answer them, though." I cross my arms over my chest, waiting for him to speak.

"Kallum," London sings, her voice light and airy as she strides into the room naked. The wooden floor creaks beneath her bare feet. Suddenly, she halts, her confident demeanor faltering as her eyes lock onto Detective Broussard. The mixture of confusion and surprise quickly tightens her brow. "Mr. Harrison?" she questions, her voice tinged with uncertainty now, a stark contrast to the playful melody she had sung moments before.

The air is charged.

The detective turns slowly toward London and laughs.

A shiver runs down my spine.

That laugh.

It's familiar.

It can't be.

He's dead.

Broussard draws a gun, swinging it toward my woman before I can react.

The detective laughs again. "You fucking bikers are all the same," he sneers. "But I didn't think it would be *this easy.*" He keeps his gun aimed at London and his eyes on me.

I'm staring at the ghost himself.

The puppeteer.

The motherfucker behind all of it.

Velasco himself.

I move.

"Take another step, she dies," he warns.

My woman stands there, staring down the barrel of a gun, naked and unflinching.

"But, then again, she's worth more to me breathing." He flicks the gun from her to me, but I don't flinch. "Too bad you put those bullets in the wrong body last night. You see, Tito was loyal. But he was also greedy and started skimming off the top." The bastard grins. "He made good bait. Thanks for saving me the trouble."

The air in the room shifts. Heavier. Colder. But the heat in my chest is nuclear.

"You think I'm afraid of death?" I growl. "You came after my family. Make no mistake, I'll take you to hell with me."

Velasco's jaw ticks. *Good. I'm getting under his skin.*

"On your knees like the dog you are," he snaps. "Now, or I put a bullet through the bitch's throat."

I drop to one knee.

"I'll gut every one of you. Your women. Your club. The King Legacy," Velasco seethes, fixated on me, on wanting to see me bleed. "All of you will pay for my father's death."

Velasco doesn't see London moving.

Then the shot.

The blast echoes like a thunderclap.

A thick spray slaps across my face, warm and metallic, the bullet punching through Velasco's forehead. He drops like a dead weight, his gun clattering across the floor.

Then...

... silence.

London locks her eyes on mine, fierce and unyielding. "I wasn't about to let that piece of shit put a bullet in my man," she growls, her gaze burning down at Velasco. "This was for Catcher too," she adds, her voice steady yet laced with adrenaline as she slowly lowers the weapon.

I push myself off the floor and close the distance between us.

I can't believe she's mine.

And at this moment, I know with every bone in my body, London is my ride-or-die.

My future.
And one day, I'm going to fucking marry her.

18

LONDON

"Anyone else notice how the guys suddenly don't look upset anymore about being here?" Luna signs.

Every head at the table turns. Sitting at the bar across the room are Kallum, Riggs, Kiwi, Nova, Wick, and Fender. Journey took the stage moments ago, and six sets of eyes are currently watching her performance.

"Why is it every time a man sees boobs, it's like they are seeing them for the first time?" Jo rolls her eyes.

Piper takes a sip of her fruity cocktail. "And to think they didn't even want to come tonight."

Piper is right. We women banded together this morning and declared tonight was girls' night, and we were spending it at Pink Paradise. The guys grumbled like a bunch of toddlers, but in the end, we got our way. Tonight is also the first night I have been back since I was tased and kidnapped in the parking lot. That was nearly three months ago, and not much has changed.

Tony had to invest in new furniture after the place was trashed, and he hired two new dancers to replace Amara and me. Everyone at Pink Paradise has rallied around Amara these past few months,

Tony especially. When I tell you Tony takes care of his girls, I mean that in every sense. Not only does Tony take care of her hospital bills, but he also pays for her counseling. Tony will cover the cost of her school tuition when she's ready to return. For now, she is taking the remainder of the semester off to focus on healing and mental health.

As for me, life has returned to normal. Work is steady and keeps me busy. Things with Kallum couldn't be better. He's broody and bossy, and I still push his buttons by tossing my sass around, which he loves. And more importantly, Mom is good. She still has her bad days, but we get through them. I cherish the good days I have with her. In fact, she has been doing so well that I can take her out from time to time. Sometimes we go to the park and have lunch, and sometimes we go for ice cream. Kallum joins us when he can. He's completely won over my mom. Her face lights up whenever he visits. I think she mostly likes to see me happy. She never said it, but she used to worry about me. She worried about leaving me alone in this world. It had always been my mom and me against the world. She was my sidekick, and I was hers. That worry I used to see in her eyes is now gone. Kallum has brought peace to my life and given my mom the same. For that, I will forever be grateful.

"Hey, London," Promise shouts over the loud music. "Why don't you get up on stage and show us some moves?"

I laugh when the other girls clap their hands and whistle. My friends were not joking the other week when they said they wanted me to teach them some moves.

"No fuckin' way," Tony says, walking past our table. "I just got all new shit in here. I let you get on that stage and shake your ass, your man will start a riot like he did last time because there will be some asshole who thinks they can put hands on you."

"Aw, Tony." I pout. "You're no fun."

"Fun my ass. "It's bad enough I gotta keep watch on you ladies tonight because you all got every hot-blooded man in here waggin' their tongues. If one of your fellas starts shootin', I'm holdin' you personally responsible." Tony points a finger at me.

"But the girls want me to show them some of my moves."

"London, quit bein' a pain in my ass."

"You love me, Tony. Admit it."

Tony puts a hand on his hip and sighs. "Tell ya what. You and your posse can come by any time before the club opens."

"Whoo hoo!" Tequila holds her shot glass up. "I like you, Tony."

"Jesus Christ," Tony mutters as he walks away. "I can tell everyone of ya are gonna be a pain in my ass."

"Babe." Kallum comes up behind me and kisses the back of my neck, causing my skin to prickle. I tip my head back and smile up at him.

"You givin' Tony a hard time?" He smirks.

I bite my bottom lip. "Yes, but that's what I do. He secretly loves it."

"You're probably right."

"I know I'm right," I counter.

Kallum tugs on my ponytail. "How drunk are you?"

"Drunk."

"Too drunk to get on the back of my bike and hold on?" he asks.

I shake my head. "I'm never too drunk to hold on."

Kallum's eyes turn heated. "Tell your girls bye." He reaches into his pocket, pulls out a few bills, and tosses the cash onto the table.

Standing, I grab my purse.

"Are you leaving already?" Promise asks.

"Yeah. I'm out, but I'll see you tomorrow."

Taking my hand in his, Kallum walks me out of the club and over to his bike. Once he's seated, I climb on behind him and wrap my arms around his waist. Closing my eyes, I breathe in his familiar scent. One would think being back here would be hard, but having Kallum and being surrounded by his warmth grounds me. He's become my peace.

Pulling out of the parking lot, Kallum heads West toward New Orleans. Twenty miles in, I notice him taking us on a detour away from the bar. I press my mouth close to his ear. "Where are we going?"

"I want to show you something?" he yells over the roaring sound of his bike. I'm confused when he starts leading us toward Riggs and Luna's house, but then he takes a left turn about a mile before their driveway and heads down a dirt road. It's pitch black with no streetlights. The only thing illuminating our path is the headlight of the motorcycle. I'm not typically a wuss, but there is something creepy about being in the woods after dark. I don't know what Kallum is up to, bringing me out in the middle of nowhere at night. A few seconds later, the bike starts to slow, and we come up on a large clearing of raw land, and I gasp when I see the city lights illuminating a massive lake in the distance. Kallum cuts the engine, and I hop off the bike.

"What is this place?" I start walking toward the edge of the lake.

I feel Kallum's heat on my back just before he wraps his arms around me from behind. "It's ours."

I turn in his arms. "What?"

"It's ours. I bought it. A few acres."

"You bought us land?" I ask, stunned.

He tucks a strand of hair behind my ear. "Yes. I want to build us a house here."

My mouth goes dry. *He wants to build us a house here.* Did I hear him right?

When I don't say anything, he continues, "I love you, London, and want to build a life with you."

Tears stream down my face. "You're serious?"

"I've never been more serious about anything in my life," he says with conviction. "What do you say, baby. Can you see yourself building a life with me?"

"Yes," I croak. "Yes, Kallum, I love you with all I am and want to spend every day by your side."

EPILOGUE
EVEREST

The sun is starting to dip behind the cypress trees lining the back of Pop's property. A few yards away, the old man throws another log into his old smoker as heavy smoke drifts on the breeze, carrying the smell of hickory. A few feet away, Riggs and Nova are manning the crawfish pots.

I'm standing on the porch, taking it all in, with a cold beer and sweat sliding down my neck. It's loud with laughter and chatter, but beneath all the noise is something quieter. Peace.

And it's been a hell of a road getting here.

The Velasco bloodline is dead.

We made damn sure of that this time.

The ghost of a man who watched every move we made after his father's death is nothing more than a bloodstain in my memory.

But today isn't about all that.

Today is for living.

For breathing easy.

The last few months have crawled and flown by in the strangest way. Some days, it feels like I just watched Velasco take his last breath yesterday. On other days, it feels as if it was a lifetime ago. I still get an itch at the base of my spine sometimes, that feeling like a storm is brewing, even when I know the threat is gone.

And through it all, my woman didn't just survive being taken and put through hell twice, she burned through it and came out on the other side stronger and still filled full of that fire and sass that makes her who she is.

We've been building something real since then. And I don't just mean the time spent behind closed doors. It's more than that.

A while back, I bought some land just outside the city, several acres of quiet, bordered by woods, with a small lake. It's peaceful out there. Wild and untamed land. The kind of place that muffles the world. And ever since, we've been sketching ideas, dreaming out loud, and watching the bones of our future take shape.

And fuck, if that doesn't scare the hell of me in the best possible way.

I'm halfway through a pile of crawfish, potatoes, and corn an hour later when I hear a vehicle coming down Pop's long driveway. A dark sedan pulls up slowly. I glance at my woman, and she's noticed the car too. The driver steps out, walks around to the passenger side, opens the door, and her mom, Faye, steps out.

"Mom?" London says, her voice mixed with surprise and confusion. She moves fast, jogging across the yard toward her, and I sit back, watching them embrace. "How are you here?" London asks her mom as they walk back slowly with Faye's nurse, Mary.

"Kallum set it all up, sweetheart." Faye winks at me.

Mary steps up. "Since she is having a good day, her doctor approved a day pass."

Getting Faye out here was a long shot because there's no way of predicting which days will be good. Alzheimer's is a fucking cruel disease, and since being with London, I've witnessed what it can do. But right now, her mother knows who she is and where she is. And that's what truly matters.

Faye scans the table, then looks around the yard, taking in all the unknown faces she has around her. "So, these are the outlaws I've been hearing about?"

Promise laughs, walks up, and hugs Faye. "In-laws, if Everest plays his cards right." She pulls back. "It's good to see you."

Faye smiles at Promise and touches her cheek. "It's good to see you too."

London leads her mom around, introducing her to our family. They invite Faye into the mix with open arms as if her being here has always been this way. Luna offers Faye a chair, and Tequila pours her a cold glass of sweet tea.

I watch the moment unfold, grateful that my woman and her mom are creating a new memory London will have to hold on to.

And all I can think about is that this, right here, is what life is all about.

This is what we fight for.

What we sacrifice for.

I get up to grab a beer when I hear another engine rolling up the dirt drive, a white SUV this time. It stops at the edge of the grass. The driver's door opens, and out steps my old man, tall, broad, with gray hair and full of grit, dressed like he just stepped out of his garage back home. He shades his eyes, scanning the yard, until he spots me. Then the passenger side opens, and my mom climbs out, wearing a bright, big smile, one I haven't seen in a year outside of FaceTime.

"What the hell..." I smile and look back at my woman.

Her smile says everything. She did this.

I cross the yard and wrap my mom in a hug that damn near breaks something in my chest.

"Kallum, sweetie, I can't breathe," Mom squeaks.

I loosen my hold and look down at her beautiful face. "What are you doin' here?"

"That beautiful woman of yours flew us out." Mom's face beams with excitement, her voice thick with emotion.

Dad grabs my shoulder, rough and solid like always. "You look good, Son."

I pull him in for a hug, and he pats my back. "Missed you, Pop."

My old man clears his throat. "Missed you too, Son."

I stand there for a beat, just my parents and me, grounded by the people who made me. And I have one person to thank for it. I turn, locking eyes with London, who is walking toward us. When she's within arm's reach, I pull her into me. "Thank you."

She shrugs, wearing a smile. "Figured you could use a reminder of home before you start building our own."

I kiss her forehead. "You know how much you mean to me, right, babe?" I pull back, staring at her for a beat, still amazed that she's mine.

London grins. "You're so obsessed with me," she teases.

I pull her tighter against my chest. "Damn right, I am. And ya know what else?"

London laughs. "What?"

"I'm gonna marry you one day." The words come out before I can stop them.

She stares at me and, without hesitating, says, "Damn right you are."

We're all sitting together, table covered in empty crawfish shells and empty beer bottles as the sun sinks into the bayou. The sounds of nature fill the air with the rhythmic chirping of cicadas, mixing with the occasional frogs croaking from the trees. A soft breeze blows, bringing the earthy smell of damp soil and adding to the peaceful feel of a moment filled with laughter and conversation.

Riggs stands, lifting his beer, and everyone quiets down. His eyes sweep the table full of people who have bled together, buried together, and stood through fire together. "We all came out here to eat, drink, and raise a little hell," he begins. "But there's another reason I wanted the family together today." He glances down at the end of the table. "Catcher," Riggs says. "Since day one, you've taken everything we've thrown at ya without bitchin' or backin' down. You've been through hell and back, even died for a minute. You spent weeks in the hospital clawing your way back. And through it all, you never stopped believing in what this patch means."

He places his drink down, reaches under the table, and pulls up a new cut with fresh stitching, 'KINGS OF RETRIBUTION MC LOUISIANA.' Then Riggs looks right at me. Typically, this is the club president's job, but this time, Riggs gives me the floor, allowing me to have the honor.

My throat becomes tight as I stand and take the cut from him. It feels heavier than anything I've ever held as I walk to Catcher, who is already pushing himself up, still sore, still healing. I slide the cut over his shoulders. "You didn't hesitate lookin' death in the eyes to save the woman I love," I tell him. "You bled for her, for the club. You've earned this."

Catcher stands tall, swallowing hard.

I pull him in for a hug, clapping him on the back. "Thank you, brother."

The yard erupts with cheers, chanting "Catcher," and bottles banging against the table's surface.

Catcher wipes a hand over his face, brushing away the emotion.

But we all see it.

We all feel it.

Family ain't just blood.

Sometimes, it's the man who nearly dies protecting what you love most.

It's the ones who bleed for the club.

The brother who rides and dies beside you.

That man is...

Kings of Retribution.